Forever Hungry

A Far Horizons Press Anthology

Far Horizons Press

FAR HORIZONS is a FREE eMagazine, brought about from a simple idea to let unpublished, thinly published and self-published writers and artists showcase their work to the World.

The first issue was released on the 17th of April, 2014.

Far Horizons Press grew out of the magazine with a desire to bring the very best stories into print. Far Horizons Press titles are designed to provide a much needed income stream so we can continue to offer the magazine free of charge and continue to develop our writers and artists.

Forever Hungry

Edited by

Pete Sutton and Kimberly Nugent

Far Horizons Press

Forever Hungry
Edited by Pete Sutton and Kimberly Nugent
Published by Stacey Welsh
Cover art Cover photos purchased from depositphotos.com
designed by SJR cover design
First Edition Published
by Far Horizons Press
25 Jul 2015
This edition TBC

This is a work of fiction. Names, places and incidents
are either products of the authors' imaginations or used
ficticiously. Any resemblences to actual persons, living or
dead (except for satirical purposes) is entirely coincidental.

Visit our website

CONTENTS

The Real Monsters

Zombie Baby

Zombie Weird

Life Lessons

Forever Hungry

Zombies...

Yes, they're disgusting, horrific to look at, smell bad, have a less-than-sunny disposition and a taste for human flesh, in particular the brain.

But we love them. For good, bad or grey-matter stuck between their teeth, we love them.

Within these gore-splattered pages, you'll find twenty-eight stories filled with the shuffling, shambling and rotting undead... and some not-quite-so-undead. All written by talented authors from all walks (and shuffles) of life.

Far Horizons Press is proud to bring you our Zombie Anthology...

Forever Hungry.

Introduction

By Pete Sutton

The word 'zombie' was first recorded in 1819 and has a long and complex literary history. Of course what made the zombie really popular was Romero's *Night of the Living Dead* and the zombie has continued to evolve as successive writers have spun the tropes in ever different and interesting ways. Zombification has been caused by a myriad of different agents, be it voodoo or genetically engineered viruses or fungi. And there seems no stopping the popularity of zombie stories. From *Night of the Living Dead* to *World War Z*, zombie films seem to be box office gold. From *I am Legend* to *Pontypool Changes Everything* to *The Girl with All the Gifts* to *The Walking Dead* (comic & TV show), they make for a very compelling story that people never tire of reading, viewing or experiencing. The popularity of zombie experiences, zombie walks and the like show that zombies have become a mainstay of the horror genre.

Here at Far Horizons our most popular issue, by a long way, was our zombie special – **http://bit.ly/1ZIby8d** and so, when we were thinking of what to do for anthologies, our minds naturally turned to the walking dead.

Our call was for zombie stories, simple as that, and we think you'll find in these pages a wide variety of takes on the subject.

In part one – Zombies, Zombies, Zombies! – you'll find our rotten friends in their most recognisable state. Tales of the zombie horde abound, but we think the ones here are some of the best you'll find.

In part two – I, Zombie – we mostly see things from the zombie's perspective. What do our rotten-brained shambling corpses think about? Do they think?

In part three – Zombies on Film – our authors explicitly wonder what would happen if the worlds of film and zombie collided, and we're not talking *Dawn of the Dead* here!

In part four – The Real Monsters – zombies are not the only thing you need to worry about in the post-zombie apocalypse world.

In part five – Zombie Baby – our writers explore what childbirth in the land of groaning, shuffling undead is like.

In part six – Zombie Weird – our writers explore various non-standard storytelling or explore the weird side of zombies.

And in part seven – Life Lessons – there are lessons to be learnt when dealing with those hungry for brains.

The zombie apocalypse, where civilisation is brought low by a zombie plague, is now deeply embedded in our culture. There are a great many films (both low and high budget), games, novels and comics about the zombie that it's obvious that the zombie trope fulfils a deep function. Many have posited it is a metaphor for disease in general, others that it is a metaphor for crime, still others that it is a metaphor for mental health.

Whatever it is, it makes for a great story and we believe that you'll find many within these covers.

It is hard to restrain oneself from extolling the virtues of each and every story and also hard to pick and choose various to promote, as it seems unfair to single any out.

Needless to say you will read many stories from different times of the zombie apocalypse. You can read about zombie babies, zombie steeds, zombie lovers and more. Zombies hunger after brains, after freedom and after love. There are poems, flash and epistolary stories as well as your more traditional short.

So sit back, relax, pour your favourite tipple and make sure all the doors and windows are locked as you enter the world of the Zombie!

Zombies, Zombies, Zombies!

Decay

By Eric Kruger

The one thing you never get used to is the screaming. The smell is so awful most people throw up the first few times, but the screaming is torture. It sounds exactly the way you think it would. Imagine someone slowly dying and their flesh falling from their bones while they are still alive. Now imagine them screaming through that pain. I don't have to imagine it. I am hearing it right now. Inside the small room everyone is trying to stay sane, but the screaming is overwhelming every thought. Sleep is almost impossible. We haven't eaten in two days and our water is all but gone. Four days ago we thought we were lucky to have escaped our previous ordeal, but we counted our chickens too early. Within minutes we were surrounded and had to run for our lives. We barricaded ourselves into the first seemingly suitable shack. There was no time to replenish our reserves or scout the area. They caught us at our most vulnerable. At first we thought we might have eluded them, as it was quiet for what seemed like an eternity. But the screaming started to build and has not stopped. Looking around the room I can see it written on everyone's faces – the end is near.

Waiting it out and not doing anything was so frustrating in the beginning. A lot of people died because they thought they were heroes. Everyone wanted to step up and save the world. A lot of people died. The authorities tried to stop the infected from harming others by deadly force. It looked like it might work for a while, but they couldn't be everywhere all the time and people took matters into their own hands. Suddenly neighbours shot each other for having the flu. Total anarchy ensued. Some people tried to ride it out, some just ran and others just disappeared. Nothing of the lives we knew was left. Cities were burning, people were dying and corpses were walking the street.

"We just need to stick it out for one more day," I try to say with confidence. Sam just looks at me. He hasn't spoken in two days. At 71 he is the oldest one of us and also the weakest. Looking at Sam I know he is not coming with us this time. Next to Sam Julie is trying to sleep. Her eyes are closed but every time the screaming reaches a fever pitch she twitches.

***

When I met Sam and Julie a month ago, I thought they were father and daughter. The way Julie was taking care of him and the way he was trying to protect her would have fooled anyone. I was alone at the time and running for my life. I ran into the back of a small house just as they ran into the front. We almost collided. We immediately realised we were all clean and started to run up the stairs. Before we even got to the rooms upstairs, the smell of decaying flesh filled the house.

The smell of death, so thick you could feel it forcing its way down your throat, choking you. Sam and Julie reached the room first and I glanced back just before they slammed the door behind me. Four corpses were coming up the stairs, dropping their flesh as they went along. The first one looked the freshest and was still pretty much intact. It couldn't have been more than a day old. Its skin was still tight from the bloating and there was no visible fluid leaking. The three behind it were pretty old, maybe three days. They had lost most of their faces and were moving pretty slowly. They didn't have much time left. Within a day they would be decomposed to a state of slush and bones on the carpet. The fresh one was the problem. If there was no escape route, we would be stuck here for at least three more days. I always carried enough supplies on me to cover me for five days, but I did not know what Sam and Julia had on them or how well prepared they were. I totally underestimated them.

Mark is sitting with his hands on his ears, rocking to and fro. It sounds like he is singing to himself, but I can't be sure. The screaming is getting pretty loud again, which is good. The louder they scream the closer they are to the end.

I walk over to Sam and give him some of my last water. "Here Sam, drink some water. We'll get out of here tomorrow. Then I'll refill my bottle." Sam's eyes say thanks, but his cracked lips are silent. Julie takes the bottle from me and gives some water to Sam. I owe Sam my life and hate to see him die like this.

***

The moment the door slammed shut Julie and Sam were running through the room grabbing the bed and some boxes to barricade the door. They didn't say a word, yet worked as one. When the door was secured Sam went to the window and locked it. Julie came over to me. "My name is Julie and that's Sam. Did any of those creeps touch you?" I know what she was getting at and why we haven't made a run for it yet. A new corpse is a big threat, since it has all the strength of the person it was, without any restraint. If they bit or scratched me, I would die within twelve hours and be up and chasing humans again in another two. If Julie and Sam where still in my vicinity, I would be a threat to them. "No, they didn't put a finger on me. You guys?" Sam just ignored my question and spoke to Julie. "So, it's getting pretty dark. We are pretty secure here. We have enough provisions. I say we wait till daylight and decide then if we stay or bail."

So we waited. Sam was pretty quiet, but Julie talked all night. I think she tried to drown out the corpse at the door, but I enjoyed the company anyway. She and Sam were not related, but met up about three months ago. Sam saw three corpses trying to get into a building screaming their heads off. He knew something was up. He locked himself up in the house across the road and saw them break through the door. He yelled through the window and threw stuff at them until they started to bang on his door. He saw a pretty girl run from the house right into the one next door. Sam thought that it was a pretty smart move from the girl, considering that night was falling. Two days later Sam and Julie formally met.

***

I realise that Mark is not singing. At first I think he's just humming, but then I start to hear the words 'idonwannadie, idonwannadie, idonwannadie,' over and over again. I go and sit next to Mark. He keeps rocking, but glances up at me. "Hey. You ready to get out of here in a few hours?" I try to sound as relaxed as possible. Mark looks at me with his big puffy face. "You reckon we's be out here soon?" The only reason Mark is still alive is because of his size. I have seen him throw a corpse across a room, splattering it against a wall. I don't think he can even read or write, but right now that is not a skill anyone can use; throwing corpses five metres through the air is. Soon we'll rely on him again.

***

After two days Sam, Julie and I left our safe room. There were a total of four corpses piled up outside the door. We treaded carefully around the sticky pile of decomposing flesh, making sure not to touch any. As careful as I was, I slipped on a bone and started to fall. Hitting the ground, breaking my skin and touching the corpses remaining fluids would be a death sentence. I felt my feet starting to give away under me and gravity claiming my body. As quickly as it was happening I was thinking what a dumb way it was to go. I have transformed myself from a geeky bookworm to a survivalist who could look after himself and help those he met. Countless times I surprised myself with my new-found strength and cunning. And although the end of the world was looming, I was rising above it. Or so I thought, until I stepped on a stupid, dumb shiny bone. Death by tripping. I felt my body hitting the ground, but it was at an awkward angle. Something was wrong. I opened my eyes and realised I was lying against the wall next to the pile of deadly remains. Sam was bracing himself against the opposite wall. Julie was looking at me with bewildered eyes. "Huh?" I uttered in disbelief, not comprehending my victory over fate. "Sam, you ok?" Julie asked. He was holding his wrist. "Yeah yeah. Tell your boyfriend to keep his eyes open." Sam started down the stairs. "I'm not sure what just happened," I admitted to Julie. "I think Sam just saved your ass. He pushed you away from the gunk as you were falling."

***

Sunlight is creeping in through the cracks in our barricades. We will have to do something now. Sam is lying way too still and Mark has stopped rocking. All is quiet inside and out. We will have to do something now. I shuffle over to Sam and Julie. I touch his arm. It is too cold. Julie just looks at me with no life in her eyes. What I am about to do will save us and make her hate me forever. I crawl over to Mark. "Hey Mark, it's time to get out of here. I will need you to do me a favour. Will you help me?" He just nods slowly. Outside I can still hear them scratching against the walls. I am getting dehydrated and my head is pounding. We will have to do something now.

***

The three of us were together for a month when we saw Mark. He was sitting on a park bench. We assumed it was a corpse, but we kept an eye on him for an hour without noticing any movement. We decided to go and inspect him up close. Sam said to let him be, but we were curious. As we got close we heard him hum and realised we made a huge mistake. In front of him, hidden from our vantage point, were about six corpses scattered on the ground. Just as we turned to run he looked up, and as if nothing could be more normal said, "I'm Mark. Are you gonna try to bite me?" I laughed for the first time in months.

***

"Julie, we need to go now. I know you love Sam, but he's not with us anymore. But he is still going to help us. Even now he is still going to help you live." Julie looks at me as if I am talking in another language. I swallow hard, but my throat just closes up more. Sam is dead and we need to get out, now. "Julie I am going to do something you are not going

18

to like and I need you to be strong and run when I say run and not turn around. You have to promise me that you will do that. For Sam." Her eyes are confused, but she nods her head yes. I stand up on weak legs and shuffle over to Mark. I already told him the plan and he knows what to do. I squeeze his arm and we walk over to Julie and Sam. Mark bends down and picks up Sam's body. Tears start to run down Julie's face. I walk her over to the furthest door away from Mark and Sam. I nod at Mark and he turns away from us, facing the window. The corpses are screaming again. Julie joins them as Mark lifts Sam's body and throws it through the window. The corpses run towards it and start to tear the flesh from his frail body. I grab Julie and we run as fast as we possibly can.

Mind the Gap

By Melanie Waghorne

Gordon hated being a commuter. To him the tube was a congealing porridge of hate to be survived every day. He hated being crammed together with strangers like some sweaty game of human Tetris. He abhorred the feeling of a handbag forced into the small of his back, the grind of a stranger against him with the sway and the swell of the train. Gordon was brimming over with passive aggression. *I'm not a scratching post you fat sow,* he thought acidly, shifting his weight from foot to foot to alleviate some of the weight of the behemoth woman leaning on his back. *The fact I am scratching my own leg and touching yours should be hint enough to get off me,* he tried to project. He scrutinized the man with his legs spread-eagled next to him. *He must have balls the size of an elephant if he needs that much room.* He couldn't see individuals any more, it was only a sea of elbows, armpits and arses, all pushed in his face, rubbed down his arm, plonked on his hand.

If the cram of the inside of the train was horrendous, Gordon's mood was not improved by the arrival at his stop. Pulled along with the swarm of faceless workers as the doors opened, he had to weave and squeeze and thrust to get to, and through, the tiny ticket barriers. Caught in the upward stream, he painfully swallowed the urge to boot the wheeled suitcase crushing his feet or the laboriously slow women in ridiculously painful-looking heels. He desperately sought not to make eye contact with anyone panicking in the hunt for their ticket in case he saw his own rage reflected back at him. He felt sour and sticky with ire but could only huff and tut along with the rabble, a horrible little melody of the morning journey – get out of the way, don't touch me, what are you looking at, move, move, MOVE.

The only thing that calmed Gordon to a level of just below surface simmer was the free paper. He skipped past the articles on the newest scandal of the Ruling Party/

Opposition Party/Fringe Party/Celebrity's Party. He sometimes read the letters page, feeling vindicated that there were others as angry as he about bikes in the standing space or people hogging the aisle seat. However, what he really enjoyed was the 'And now... ' piece. It cheered him to read about the bear doing yoga, the dog having the birthday party, or the duck seemingly shopping in an off-licence. For a little while at least, he felt less acerbic, less like screaming into the faces of his fellow travellers. Gordon had saved today's paper for the trip home. He was gratefully losing himself in a story of a man assembling a ghoulish Sylvanian family out of taxidermy mice. So much so he did not notice the man in the crumpled and stained suit lurch onto his carriage. He might not have seen him at all if the shuffling man's shoe had not connected sharply with Gordon's ankle. Gordon bit back a shout of indignation; this particular 'suit' looked rough, and he didn't much want to round off his day with a punch on the nose.

Gordon watched him meander down the centre aisle, kicking bags and feet in turn as he made his unsteady way down the carriage. He seemed to have blood staining a shirt cuff and dripping down his fingers. Maybe someone had already received that punch, thought Gordon, relieved that the inebriated man hadn't sat down next to him. Gordon winced as the train pulled away from the station, he watched the tottering drunk lose his battle with gravity, crashing noisily backwards onto the sticky floor. A collective cry came up from the sardined commuters, much like the hissed intake of breath when a barmaid drops a tray of glasses. Gordon heard a few titters until it was obvious that the man wasn't getting up.

No one wanted to get involved. Londoners are pathologically afraid of having to touch anyone, especially a sloshed investment banker, maybe raring for a fight. Gordon certainly wasn't going to get up – he hadn't got a seat on the way home for a week, and he wasn't going to surrender it for anyone, certainly not someone he thought was probably potted on champagne worth more than Gordon's monthly ticket. Finally a labourer, looking around in indignation at his fellow travellers, most of whom had started to find the eye-height adverts very interesting, walked up to the prone man.

"You alright mate?" he shouted down at him with the forced camaraderie of a man who didn't really want to be involved but thought that he should anyway.

"Hello?" Silence. He waited a beat. "Oi mate."

The labourer leaned down and shook the prostrate figure. His head wobbled, crunching against the laminate surface.

"Shit." The builder felt around in the man's collar, a panicked expression growing on his face, hunting desperately for the slow, thick thud of an unconscious pulse.

"He's fucking dead."

"He can't be. Look. Move!" A frumpy woman in a too-tight suit pushed the labourer out of the way. She went to cup his wrist for the ulnar pulse but dropped it quickly, her hands slick with blood. Gordon could see a semi-circle of flesh missing from the man's forearm. Everyone was rapt on the drama playing out, like motorists crawling past the scene of a crash, hoping to see a smear of blood on the black top.

The woman stood, wiping her bloodied hands down her bulging skirt, her face a mask of shock.

"Told you," the labourer complained, like a petulant child.

"Pull the alarm," she whispered.

He did, heaving the red lever down. An angry voice squawked from the intercom, but like any other driver announcement it was unintelligible. The frumpy suited woman, now looking decidedly green, managed to shout a few words back into the speaker, "Dead! Blood! HELP!" That seemed to be enough for the driver, and without warning the brakes began to squeal, the force dragging the carriages and making them lurch. Everyone screamed as the carriage swung, throwing people from their seats, sliding the body a few feet down the walkway towards Gordon.

As the train halted, rolling a little on the tracks, Gordon found himself transfixed by the sheen of the fluorescent lights on the staring eye of the dead man. He couldn't drag his gaze away, an ugly voyeur like everyone else, a rubbernecker unable to help. He'd never seen anyone dead before. Funny, wasn't it? That one moment... his rumination was cut short as the glassy eye began to roll wildly in its socket, spinning like a marble, eyelids flickering as fast as a bird's wing.

The dead man's arm flicked out, clamping around the frumpy woman's wrist, pulling her down whisper-quick into an embrace from rapidly cooling arms. A scream died in her throat as his teeth found her neck, nuzzling into her like an infant. Gordon heard the cracking of tendons, like chicken bones, as arterial spray spurted onto the train windows, streaking through the grime, sprinkling the horrified travellers like a water-park ride.

Gordon heaved to his feet, the newspaper sloughing from his grip like peeling skin. The tube carriage had erupted into a cacophony of screams, but underneath the bedlam, he could still hear the cadaver's slurping, like a child trying to reach the last of a milkshake through a straw. Gordon gawked as the suited man began to pull himself up, knees slipping in the syrupy blood. His mind fluttered against a long forgotten image, a children's TV programme with celebrities slipping in gunge. The recently re-animated corpse had dropped the depleted body, but even as it gained its feet he could see the murdered woman's hand begin to twitch, clawing patterns into the mire.

"Move, move, MOVE!" Gordon yelled as he hurled himself through the carriage, away from that noise, away from death in a suit.

Gordon fought, squeezed and wiggled through the heaving

mass of bodies, a squirming mess of worms in a bait bucket. Moving towards the interconnecting doors, he shoved himself past a flawlessly made up woman shredding her shellac manicure on the closed doors and a boy trying to slither through the tiny tube window, caught like a cat in a flap. Bile squirted hot and sour into the back of his throat as he realised the shifting weight under his feet was a carpet of people. He looked down to see the heel of his highly polished shoe crunch into the temple of a uniformed woman, cracking it like the shell of a hardboiled egg.

Panting and slick with sweat, Gordon slammed against the last door at the end of the train, the handle connecting solidly with his stomach. *That'll bruise tomorrow,* he thought, letting out a small shrill bark of laughter at the absurdity of it. He struggled desperately with the mechanism of the door, fear and sweat making his hands clumsy. *Oh Jesus, Oh God, Oh help me, Oh ughmf.* The drop from the carriage to the dirt floor of the tunnel was longer than he expected. He could feel grit in his eyes and mouth.

Several other bodies tumbled out of the door with him and Gordon smelled a thick, smoky BBQ smell as a bespectacled woman hit the third rail. He watched her twitch and jive spasmodically, her skin smouldering and melting onto the grill of the electrified steel. He goggled as she tried to pull her rendered face away, most of it adhering to the surface, an eye spilling down her cheek. He stumbled to his feet, skidding slightly on the loose rocks, and begun to run blindly back into the tunnel. Behind him the train was a myriad of wails, layered with the nursing suck of the dead feasting on the living.

As Gordon hurried away from the stricken train the light started to dissipate, slowly at first, but soon he was running full pelt into the midnight black of the tunnel. His nerves jangled and screamed at the total sensory deprivation. How every foot fall and beat of his heart reverberated in his ears. *It hadn't been that long since they left the last station, had it?* Gordon had no idea how much time had passed on his stumbling run through the dark, he had only been anchored somewhat by running his hand along the tunnel wall, trying to keep himself away from the rails. He could still smell the smouldering girl, could see the after-image of her cooked visage before him. His breath came out in tiny sobs, expecting a cold hand to tear at his shoulder or ankle, hearing the wailing, screaming and slurping of death behind him. His side had begun to constrict painfully with a stitch, a tangled elastic band growing tighter under his flesh.

Light was starting to bleed through the darkness from an illuminated station just beyond the mouth of the tunnel. Gordon cried out in relief when his sore, grazed fingers bumped into the rim of a poster at the entrance. He was blind at the sudden light but heard the clamour his emergence had caused on the platform. He lumbered forward like a spectre, face smeared with blood, soot and fear as he babbled and screeched, his stitch and panic crushing the words in his mouth.

Two men on the edge of the platform hunkered down to him, gesturing wildly for Gordon to come towards them; he couldn't make out their words, just the fish-like opening and closing of their mouths. Why couldn't he hear them? Why was it so loud? *Oh fuck.* He could feel the reverberation of a train barrelling towards him.

Gordon leapt over the rails, the toes of his shoes catching on the innermost rail, making him stumble to his knees. He scrabbled his way up the platform side, shredding the skin on his fingers and knuckles. Adrenaline had drained him; his fingertips found the edge of the platform, but his arms trembled under the exertion of pulling himself up. His nails bent back and snapped, his legs fishtailed desperately against the stone. His two would-be rescuers knelt down to him, pulling at his sleeves, under his armpits, at his belt. Their hysterical see-sawing pulling was knocking his balance, pulling his hands away from their grip on the platform.

25

"Get off! Let go! STOP! PLEASE! YOU ARE GOING TO KILL ME," he hollered.

The sound of the train, its impending stampede of mechanisms, was deafening. Gordon wriggled his belly over the side, the men still pulling at his arms. Just a little further.

Gordon felt the impact of several tonnes of metal hit him, begging to drag him along with its momentum. It probably would have done so had the men still not been clinging to him. He felt his hips crumble under its weight, skin splitting and spilling its contents like rotten fruit. He sensed the separation of muscle from sinew and bone. He knew the grate of steel deep within him. He was aware of the sensation of separation. His half-body slithered onto the platform edge, his legs dropping corpulent and dripping onto the rails. He could smell the start of their sizzling.

The station crowd was a cacophony of screams and wails. They gathered around him like a fish, hooked wet and flapping onto the dock. His body felt burdensome and numb, something separate, detached from his thoughts. There was no pain from his severed spine. He was aware that someone had grabbed his grotesquely bent hand in their own, he listened absently to their mantra that everything was going to be all right. *Not bloody likely,* Gordon thought good-naturedly. His detached and fleeting consciousness managed to focus itself one last time, and it focused on a pallid hand sporting a shredded shellac manicure hooking itself over the platform edge, finger-painting in his spilled blood.

Thankfully Gordon was dead, staring unseeing at the ceiling as the miscreations began to gorge themselves on his remaining flesh. The majority of people that night were not so fortunate. The carcass army swarmed the station, tearing, feasting, multiplying. They spilled over the barriers and into the night of Piccadilly Circus, illuminated by the Coca-Cola sign, watched over by the stoic sculpture of Anteros, a halcyon observer to the end of the world.

Picnic in the Park

By Tim Jeffreys

It was the warmest day of the year so far. James said the temperature must be twenty-two degrees at least, unusual for the end of March, which is why Laura thought it strange that there was no one else in the park. In fact, she reminded herself, they hadn't seen anyone during the short walk from their house. Not even a car on the road.

James must have been thinking the same thing. After laying the picnic cloth out in the grass, he glanced around then said, "Well it is Sunday morning."

"Maybe there's something happening elsewhere," Laura said. She showed him a half-smile. "Something we don't know about."

"Always the last to know," he said. And they both laughed.

As James began to set the food and drink out on the cloth, Laura crouched to check on Scarlett who was still sleeping in her baby carrier with her little hands balled under her chin. Smiling, Laura turned the carrier a little so that Scarlett was out of the direct sunlight. Then she stood and glanced over towards the enclosed play area to see what Harry and Amelia were doing. Harry was of course in the sand pit and Amelia was climbing the ropes of the pirate ship.

"It's a shame there aren't any other children here," Laura said to James. "Harry's been stuck in front of the TV for a week and Amelia's had all that schoolwork to do. It would've been nice if they'd had someone to play with."

"Give it time," James said. He had finished setting out the picnic food. Now he sat down in the grass and opened a beer. "It's still early."

Laura looked at her watch. It was almost noon. Was that early? She supposed it was for a Sunday.

James was looking up at her, squinting against the sun at her back. He sipped his beer. "Relax. We've got the whole park to ourselves. Enjoy it."

"Hmm... I suppose you're right. Shall I call the kids over?"

"Let them play a bit."

Laura let her gaze wander around the empty park. Had the clocks gone back last night? Maybe that was it. Her watch said twelve but it was actually only eleven. Eleven was definitely early for a Sunday. But no, that wasn't right. Didn't the clocks go *forward* at this time of year?

"There'll be something going on somewhere. Like you said."

"I suppose so. But doesn't it seem... "

She let the thought trail off. With a shrug, she gave James a half-smile then sat down in the grass next to the baby carrier, reached over, and popped an olive in her mouth. James was tearing into a chicken leg as if he'd not eaten in a week. She looked away.

She enjoyed the touch of the sun on her bare arms, and she thought how glad she was that winter was behind them. Now she could start taking Scarlett out more in her pram whilst James was at work and the other two children at school. She liked to get out and about. Being stuck in the house all day made her feel so...

"What was that?" James said. Laura looked at him and saw him glance towards the play area. She looked that way herself and saw that Amelia had reached the top of the pirate ship. She was standing on the wooden ledge, looking towards her parents, and gesturing frantically with one hand. Laura realised that she could also hear her daughter shouting.

"What's wrong with her?"

"Maybe she can't get down. Stuck."

"She never got stuck before."

James stood up. He cupped his hands around his mouth and shouted to Amelia. "What's wrong? Are you stuck?"

Amelia shouted back but her voice was too far away for them to hear what she was saying.

"I'll go," Laura said.

"No wait," James said. "She's climbing down."

They watched as Amelia descended the ropes. She collected her brother from the sand pit and then the two were running heads down towards them.

"What's got into them?"

"Maybe they're just hungry. Smelt the food." James laughed. For some reason, Laura didn't feel like laughing.

The two children were out of breath by the time they reached their parents. Henry – Laura was alarmed to see – was crying. Amelia kept trying to say something but couldn't.

"Whatever's gotten into you two?" James said.

"Running!" Amelia managed at last. "Running! Lots and lots of them! I saw... from the top... of the... "

Laura crouched down and took hold of her daughter's hands. Someone was trembling. She didn't know if it was Amelia or herself, or both of them.

"What is it, darling? What did you see? Who's running?"

"Them!" Amelia said, throwing a fearful look over Laura's shoulder and pointing.

Laura turned her head.

Down the slope of the road on the far side of the park, near the entrance gates, came a crowd of people, all running.

There must have been over a hundred people. Laura stood slowly and stared.

An odd thought passed through her mind. *Well, here everyone is.*

"James... ?"

Laura looked at her husband. James swallowed, then tried a smile. "Some kind of marathon... you think?"

Laura looked back towards the crowd. It contained all kinds of people, old and young. There were even some children. Their running had a kind of desperate energy to it, as if they were not running under the force of their own will, but through some compulsion. Some compulsion like...

Like hunger.

Laura didn't know why this thought had popped into her mind. It was something about the way the crowd were scrambling down the hill. It was as if they were all searching desperately for something, each member wanting to be the first to get to it. Whatever *it* was.

As the crowd reached the bottom of the hill, a man turned his head and Laura felt her heart leap as she realised she and her family had been noticed. At once, some of the crowd broke away – following this man's lead – and were soon inside the park gates and running full pelt towards Laura and her family.

"Er... James?"

James gazed back at her with his mouth hanging open.

Laura looked down at the small pale faces of her children, and at Scarlett still fast asleep in her baby carrier.

"Mummy," Amelia said, her voice dulled by fear. "They're coming."

Revelation

By Vincent Bivona

Dean pulled on his wife's outstretched arm, trying to get her to run faster. She was falling behind, her free hand protecting the swell of her belly, her feet shuffling through broken glass and the gritty pebbles of the asphalt.

"Laura, honey, please, you have to move faster. They're right behind us."

He glanced over his shoulder, taking in their attackers. Three zombies, each of the grotesque creatures moaning, their heads canted on broken necks, saliva drooling out of their crooked mouths. They ran with the speed of gazelles and pursued with the noses of bloodhounds.

"This way, quick!"

He jerked Laura's arm, pulling her down an alleyway. They were in the 'City of the Damned,' once a heavily populated centre of commerce and culture, now a desolate wasteland quartering the poor.

Everything had changed since the outbreak. Once the first case of ZD had been reported, the electrified fence had gone up and the military had come in, breaking the city into factions. The poor were left to fend for themselves on one side, while corporate America and the rich were allowed entry into what had been deemed the 'Zone of Safety.' It didn't take long for the dichotomy to present itself. Soon the City of the Dead became a festering rat hole. All sense of order was dismissed. Electricity was terminated. Crime ran rampant. Garbage littered the streets. It regressed to a society where survival of the fittest became the fundamental decree. While on the other side of the fence, the military-guarded paradise prospered. Business continued, consumerism resumed, and construction began anew, widening the windows in the CEOs' high-rise mansions so they could look down upon the zombie-ridden faction that made their luxuriant lives

31

possible.

Dean hated the Upper Faction with all of his heart, but he knew it would be the Upper Faction who he must depend on to save his life.

"In here," he said, ushering Laura into an abandoned building. The moment she stepped foot over the threshold, he pushed her up against the wall, using his body to shield her if the zombies should follow them in. To his relief, they didn't – they stalked past the open doorway, moaning through their slavering mouths.

"That was close," he said, panting.

Laura acted as if she hadn't heard him. She was too busy staring at his forearm.

"Oh my God, Dean… "

Dean quickly pulled his arm away. "It's nothing."

Laura grabbed it, hissing through her teeth as she inspected the bleeding wound. "What are you talking about? They bit you!"

"Better me than you."

"Are you serious? What are we gonna do?"

"The Upper Faction have antidotes. We just have to get to them in time."

"You think they'll just give you an antidote?"

"I work for them, don't I?"

"You work *for* them, exactly. They don't care about their workers. They don't care about any of us. You know that!"

"Laura, I have to try! It's our only hope."

Laura struggled not to cry. "How long do you have before

you change?"

Dean popped his head out the doorway, making sure the coast was clear, and found an early warning scanner.

Before the fence had gone up and the factions were created, the solar-powered scanners had been installed all around the city as precautionary measures, the police needing to know if a victim could be safely transported to a hospital to receive the antidote to the ZD virus before he or she changed.

Dean stuck his finger under the scanner. There was a sharp prick, and the computer beeped. A second later a number flashed across its display.

"Forty-seven minutes," he said to Laura in an almost defeated tone.

The moment he said the words, her face dropped. It was a full two hours before the Zone of Safety opened their gates. Even if the Upper Faction would give Dean the antidote, he'd never get it in time.

At precisely 9 pm every night, the Zone of Safety opened their gates and awarded the poor temporary protection from the zombies in exchange for twelve hours of work, as well as a monetary pittance. There they slaved under harsh conditions, working the graveyard shift – out of sight, out of mind. They performed the types of labour none of the Upper Faction wanted to do. In the morning, they were released back into the City of the Damned, left to fend for themselves. Sometimes, because they were so tired and overworked, they got caught before they could even make it back to their shelters. Sometimes they never made it to work the next day at all. And sometimes they got chased to work by the very person they had been working with the day before, he or she not having been lucky enough to run a little faster the previous night.

Because of a technological breakthrough, the Upper

Faction didn't have any trouble allowing the residents of the City of the Damned entry. They designated a 200-foot square area in front of their gates as a loading zone and surrounded it with Hollers, electronic devices that emitted a high-pitch frequency detrimental to zombies. If one should get too close, its head would explode, splattering coagulated blood and brains every which way. All a person seeking work in the Zone of Safety had to do was arrive in the loading zone the moment the Hollers were activated, and they could wait in safety until he or she was let in half an hour later.

Unfortunately Dean didn't have the luxury of waiting.

"You only have forty-seven minutes?" Laura asked, making sure she'd heard her husband right.

Dean nodded solemnly. "That's what the scanner said."

"No... no, that can't be. What are we gonna do?"

He hugged his wife, stroking her hair as she sobbed on his shoulder. "There's not much we can do," was all he said.

***

Dean wasn't sure how much time had passed before Laura jerked her head up, a hopeful look marking her face.

"What about the outposts?"

"What about them?"

"They're guarded by the military, aren't they? They might have a supply of the antidote for the soldiers. Just in case, you know?"

Dean hadn't thought of that. A smile stretched his lips across his face, and he squeezed Laura, hard enough to show her his gratitude but not enough to harm the baby.

"Laura, you're an absolute genius! I love you!"

Laura blushed. "Maybe not a genius, but I do have a good idea from time to time."

He grabbed her hand, and together they exited the building. On the way he used the Early Warning scanner to prick his finger again.

Nineteen minutes.

"Come on, we have to get there quick! We don't have that much time!"

They wove their way through the abandoned buildings and the desolate streets, diligently listening for any sign of the zombies. There was the occasional moan in the distance and the sharp human cry that followed as a zombie gave chase, but that was all.

Dean said, "There should be an outpost around this corner."

Sure enough, he was right. Just ahead, surrounded by a fifteen foot fence lined with razor wire, was one of the outpost buildings. A large wooden sign marked the front, reading,

FOOD

WATER

&

SUPPLIES

A single halogen floodlight spilled its brilliance on the brick structure, along with the two armed guards standing against the building. Enveloped by all the darkness, it looked like a shimmering desert oasis.

Laura let out a breath she had been holding. "Thank God."

"Cross your fingers," Dean told her. "We're going to need all the luck we can get."

As they approached the building, one of the soldiers raised his machine gun, shining the attached flashlight in Dean's face.

Dean immediately thrust his hands into the air. "Don't shoot! We're—"

That was all he got out before something crashed into him from behind. The world tumbled as he collapsed to the ground. From somewhere to his side, Laura screamed. It took him only a moment to get to his feet, but it was a second too late. The zombie that had bowled him over had Laura in its deadly embrace, struggling to gnaw on her flesh.

Dean didn't waste a second. He didn't even think. Just acted. With all the strength he possessed, he flung himself at the zombie, knocking both it and Laura down. He heard her cry out the same moment an immense pain erupted in his leg.

"Kill it!" he shouted as the zombie bit down on his thigh. "Kill it!"

He had no idea who he was shouting to. Only knew that he wanted this bestial thing off him. He kicked and punched and writhed, fighting for his life. Eventually he was rewarded for his efforts as he pushed the zombie away. He held it by its neck at an arm's length, carefully avoiding its bloody mouth as it ravenously snapped at him. The energy the undead thing possessed was incredible, and he struggled to hold it still as more zombies somewhere in the distance echoed its moans.

It was a losing battle. He felt his strength ebbing and the zombie getting closer. It was maybe an inch or two away from his face when a steel pole burst out of its neck.

At first Dean didn't understand what happened, then he looked behind the zombie and saw Laura holding the other end of the pole. She dropped it the moment the zombie keeled over, and buried her face into her hands and sobbed.

Dean quickly got to his feet and wrapped his arms around his wife. He held her there, in the halogen light from the outpost building, feeling the warmth of her body and the maddening pulse of her heart.

"Thank you," he said. "Thank you so much. You saved my life. You're absolutely amazing."

Laura looked up at him, tears streaking her cheeks. "I don't think I can do this anymore. I can't live like this."

"It's okay," Dean reassured her. "It'll all be okay."

"No, it won't. Not with a baby on the way. We can't live our lives constantly running, never knowing if today might be our last."

"If today is our last," Dean said, "then I'm the luckiest man in the world to get to spend it with you."

"How touching... " said a voice.

Dean whirled around to find the soldier who had shined the light in his face now standing up against the fence. He made a puckering motion with his lips at Laura.

"Listen," said Dean, "I need the antidote. I've been bitten."

"I can see that," said the soldier, looking at the gaping wound in Dean's leg.

"No, before." Dean held out his forearm, exposing the bite. "I don't have much longer before I change."

"What makes you think we have the antidote?" said the other soldier, stepping up beside his partner.

Laura's face dropped. "You mean you don't have it?"

"Oh we have it, all right. But why would we ever give it to you?"

"Please," Laura begged. "We'll give you anything."

The soldier lustily eyed the curves of her tight figure, especially the swell of her breasts above the small bulge of her belly. "Anything?"

Laura took a cautious step back.

Dean glared at the man dressed in the camouflaged fatigues.

"I think we may be able to strike up a bargain," said the first soldier. "If your wife's willing, that is."

Laura flashed Dean a horrified look. Then she glanced at the ravaged flesh of his forearm and leg, and concern replaced repulsion. "Dean... maybe we should—"

"Forget it," he said. "What kind of husband would I be if I let you sacrifice yourself like that?"

"A dead one," replied the first solder.

"An *un*-dead one," corrected the second. "You should strongly consider our proposition. Like you said, you don't have much time left."

It turned out Dean had less time than he thought. A zombie shambled its way into the street. Followed by two more.

"Seems like our proposition's looking better by the second," said the soldier, flashing a devious smile. "What's it going to be?"

Dean looked quickly from his wife to the solder. It took all of two seconds to come up with an appropriate response.

"Go fuck yourself."

***

If living in the City of the Damned had taught Dean and Laura anything, it was how to run away from zombies.

There were certain tricks you could employ to increase your chances of survival. Like slipping in and out of buildings and climbing ladders whenever possible. There weren't too many ladders around, but Dean and Laura slipped in and out of as many abandoned buildings as they could find. Because of their efforts, they earned themselves a formidable lead on the zombies chasing them. Now, if they could only find a way to outrun the virus worming its way through Dean's bloodstream...

"We're not gonna make it," Dean said. "There's no time. There's nowhere to go."

Laura scowled at him. "Don't you say that. Don't you *ever* say that. There's still a chance."

She desperately wanted to believe herself, but with each passing moment, it seemed more and more likely that she would find herself running from her husband instead of next to him.

In the distance, a large steel gate appeared like a mirage. "There!" Dean called out, a painful hope propelling his voice. It was the Zone of Safety. The Hollers weren't activated yet, but they marked the area with their ethereal glow.

Laura yelled at the top of her lungs as they approached. "Help! Help us! For the love of God, you've got to help us!"

"Turn the Hollers on!" Dean shouted. "Please, we're being chased!"

The soldiers behind the fence regarded them like bored children who are about to be entertained.

"Don't just stand there! Do something!"

One of the soldiers folded his arms over his chest and sneered.

"Please!" Laura shouted. "My husband needs the antidote! He's been bitten. We have a baby on the way. Please!"

In response, two of the soldiers raised their guns. Laura's eyes widened.

From behind her, three zombies emerged, peeling themselves out of the darkness like shadows. They shambled forward, the monstrous leers on their faces marking their insatiable hunger.

"Looks like we're going to have ourselves quite a show, boys!" said one of the guards.

Dean flashed him the most vehement grimace he could muster. "Do something! Turn on the Hollers! Shoot them!"

The soldiers did no such thing. They kept their guns aimed but stood there like spectators, waiting for the fun to begin.

"What's wrong with you?" Laura shouted at them. "Don't any of you have a heart? A family? I'm pregnant! You can save our lives! Just shoot the zombies and give us the antidote! Quick, before it's too late!"

One of the soldiers broke off from his group and approached the gate. He pressed his face as close to the electrified fence as he dared. Laura's heart swelled as he reached into his pocket and extracted something.

This was it. They were finally going to get the antidote, and not a moment too soon.

Laura's world came crashing down when the soldier slipped what he was holding through the fence.

It was a knife.

She peered into the soldier's cold hard gaze. "It's the best I can do," he said. "It'll be less painful if you end it yourself."

"Why won't you help us?" she asked, impossible from keeping the desperation out of her voice.

His answer was clear and concise: "Because, you're on the wrong side of the fence."

That seemed to say it all. With that, Laura grudgingly accepted the knife, and the soldier stepped back. She regarded the cold polished steel of the blade. So sharp and deadly. So...

"Laura, run!"

Dean's voice snapped her out of her thoughts. In her preoccupation, she'd overlooked just how close the zombies were. Without hesitation, Dean took her by the elbow and sprinted into the darkness. "Thanks for nothing!" he shouted at the soldiers as he went.

***

Together they ran as far as their legs would carry them.

"Keep going!" Dean coached her.

A painful stitch blossomed in Laura's side, nearly crippling her. "I can't," she said. "I need to rest."

Dean snapped a quick look behind them. A rest was out of the question. "We can't, honey. They're too close."

"I can't go on," she said. "It's impossible."

Dean twisted his face in concern. They were pretty much out in the open, in the middle of the street. They had weaved their way through the City of the Damned and were in what could only be described as the 'residential district,' a set of blocks where those who lived on this side of the fence took refuge from the zombies. As dilapidated as the shelters might be, their doors would be locked or barricaded, and Dean knew the fear of being bitten would keep the people inside from opening them.

Behind him, the zombies moaned in anticipation as they drew closer to their next meal.

Dean quickly scanned the area, not really expecting to find anything, but knowing he had to try anyway. To his surprise, there was a ramshackle building housing two stores that nobody was hiding in.

"Laura, quick! In there!"

He ushered his wife into the store on the right and quickly pulled down the security gate behind her.

The instant she realized her husband wasn't joining her, she cried out. "Dean! What are you doing?"

"I didn't get the antidote. There's no way I'm going to change with you next to me."

"Dean! Get your ass in here! There's still time!"

Dean would do no such thing. Instead, he stepped into the store next to hers and pulled down its security gate. He didn't have a second to spare. As soon as he secured it, the zombies crashed into it with a thunderous crash, thrusting their arms through the gaps in the metal, reaching out for him.

Dean staggered backwards to the rear of the store, catching his breath.

"Dean!"

There was a small window in the wooden partition separating the two stores. Nothing big enough to slip through, but big enough for Laura to pop her head in one side and out the other.

"Dean! Why did you do that?"

Gradually, he got to his feet and caressed her face. "Honey, I told you. I don't have much time left."

As if to prove this, he used the Early Warning scanner on the wall to prick his finger.

Three minutes, twenty-six seconds.

"What's it say?"

"Don't worry about it. The important thing is that I love you."

That brought the tears. Dean watched them flow freely from his wife's eyes, running down her cheeks and dripping to the floor. The sight made his own eyes water, knowing that he would soon be leaving her and everything else he had ever known behind.

Although, maybe it wasn't all that bad. If he took a look back at his life, Laura was the only good that had come out of it. The rest had been meaningless. All those backbreaking hours he'd put in at work were hours that would never benefit him, but benefit the people who had refused to help him. Benefit the people who had basically *enslaved* him. If anything, he'd be free from that absurdity now. Free from that prison. The only true free ones were the zombies. They had so much vitality, so much drive, traits he hadn't possessed ever since the breakout and the dividing of the factions. It made him realize something else: those creatures running around outside, trying to devour his brains, thrusting their arms through the gaps in the security gate – they weren't the zombies. No, *he* was the zombie, imprisoned and trapped in a society with no social mobility.

"Please... " Laura said. "Don't do this to me. Don't leave me behind."

"It's okay," he told her, growing more certain with each passing second. "It'll be better to be a zombie than to continue living like this and working for the Upper Faction."

Laura's eyes widened. "What are you saying?"

"At least what the zombies do, they do for themselves, not like us, who work for the people who forced this life upon us. They could get rid of the zombies whenever they want. They could put Hollers all over the city and chase them out. But they don't. They could have opened their gates early for us. But they didn't. And they could have given me the antidote. But they didn't do that either. I'm done with them, Laura. I'm done playing their game. It's time for something different. Something better… "

Before she could argue, he pressed his lips against hers, savouring her soft touch and the warmth of her body one last time.

When he pulled away, he began to shake.

"Dean, no!"

He collapsed to the floor in a seizure. His legs and arms twitched and shook in convulsions. White foam seeped out of his mouth, dribbling to the floor.

"Dean!"

Her husband writhed in what looked like horrible pain. His back arched suddenly and violently. Finally, he grew still. After a long moment, he raised his head, his eyes cloudy and distant, empty of all emotion, an insane look of hunger transforming his features.

Still crying, Laura pulled her head back onto her side of the partition. Very slowly, she pulled out the knife the soldier had given her, remembering his words: *It's the best I can do. It'll be less painful if you end it yourself.*

She dropped her gaze to the exposed flesh of her wrist and the roadmap of veins that traced its way under her skin. Could she really let out the life that beat within those veins?

No, she couldn't. She refused to take the coward's way out. If she did, she would never be with her husband, and she had promised in sickness and in health that she would be with him always, till death did they part… and if she thought about it, there was a way she could even be with him beyond that.

44

Biting her lip, she loosened the fingers holding the knife, letting it clatter to the floor. She didn't pay it any attention. Instead, she kept her gaze focused on the small window between the stores and the familiar-looking creature on the other side furiously beating against the security gate for escape.

Using all her courage, she approached the window and extended her arm, slowly feeding her wrist through the gap. As she did, she realized she wouldn't be able to mother the child in her belly after her husband turned her. Surprisingly that didn't upset her as much as it should have. (After what he had pointed out, she didn't think it would be fair to bring a child into a world like this, anyway.) What really upset her was the cruel nature of human beings, along with the level of greed that could exist in those who had the power to fix things but chose not to because it didn't benefit them. That was the worst of all. Yet, in due time, it would be something she would never have to concern herself with again. In due time, she would finally be free.

Shipwreck

By Jackie Pitchford

I send this missive to my beloved sister, Elizabeth Marchant, on the thirteenth day of July in the year of our Lord 1826.

Dear Elizabeth,

I hope you and your family are all in good health. I am well. Justin has taken good care of me, despite our troubles.

It is for an account of those troubles, dear sister, that I take pen to paper, and may God have mercy on our souls for the writing of it.

As you know, sweet Elizabeth, we had planned to travel to Jamaica to take over Justin's inheritance of a sugar plantation. To this end we had happily embarked from Plymouth last month on our exciting journey. The Epiphany was fully laden, we struggled to fit our own cargo aboard, oh if only we had known then what we know now we would have never set out on this cursed journey.

But I digress. We floundered four days ago, and almost everyone was lost. My little dog Elsie made it ashore but not the maid, Jane. We have been fortunate in that much of the cargo has also washed ashore, and we would have been relatively comfortable awaiting our rescue had it not been for the natives.

On our second night strange noises were heard: urgent, snuffling, abhorrent sounds that were always just that little too far away to identify; Justin stood guard all night with some of the sailors. It was noted that several sailors were missing the following morning, we assumed they would return once they had gotten over their fright.

They did return, but not as sailors. Elizabeth, it pains me to write this, but the natives of this island are not living souls.

Justin has done his best to preserve us with a barrier of blessed water and a goodly supply of stakes alongside the few guns washed ashore from the ship, but there are only he and four sailors remaining and, unless a ship arrives soon, I fear our mortal lives are to come shortly to an end.

Dear sister, we remain by the grace of God in our cliff top redoubt, but I do not know how long these walls shall last against the onslaught of the zombies outside. I shall cast this missive into the ocean in the vain hope that our sorry demise shall serve as a warning to future travellers, that they may avoid this accursed isle. We cling to the hope that we shall be rescued but it seems an increasingly vain hope, a poor light in the gathering darkness.

We send our love to you and yours. Remember us, and let our tale be told,

From your beloved sister,

Joanna West

Toothless Piranhas

By Adam Gaylord

The creature's teeth cracked on my face-shield with a sickening crunch, bloody gums smearing across the safety glass. It sucked futilely, managing nothing more than to further foul my vision.

That's the thing about us humans – we're not designed to be predators. Take away our big brains and our tools and what are we left with? No claws, no fangs, no venom, no nothin'.

That's why one zombie isn't a threat. It's more of a novelty, really. Something to watch with morbid curiosity and wonder, who did it use to be? Did it have a husband? Did it have kids? Did it bring store-bought cookies to the PTA bake sale?

And physically? A puma will clear a twenty foot fence from a standstill. A grizzly will peel open your car like a can of sardines. A hyena will crush your skull like popcorn. Your average zombie can't even bite through heavy fabric.

Which is where the safety suit came from. At some point, somebody realised that a good canvas jacket went a long way toward not getting infected when running for your life. Different folks tried different additions: spray-on truck bed liner, chain-mail, armour plates, spikes, etc. Some worked, some didn't. 'Necessity's the mother' and all that. It didn't take long before the suits were pretty impenetrable.

The one I'm wearing now, for example, they can chomp on this thing all day and not make a dent. It even has its own support skeleton, to keep you from getting crushed in a horde. Our latest and greatest. Impenetrable.

Which brings me back to the poor fellow still gumming on my face shield. He's not my problem. He doesn't have the tools to open this can. Neither is his friend on my right arm,

48

nor his comrade on my left leg, nor even the fellow tearing desperately at my crotch. No, my problem is threefold. First, my current horizontal orientation. Second, the fact that, in addition to the four I just mentioned, I seem to be the main attraction at the centre of a zombie feeding frenzy several hundreds strong.

And you have to give zombies credit, what they lack in predatory adaptations they make up for in sheer persistence. I've seen a zombie claw at a locked door until its hands were worn down to nubs. Which is the final piece of my doom puzzle, ol' gummy and his friends aren't going to give up. I'm stuck here. For good.

Panic was hours ago, after I was first taken down. Since then is a little hazy. There was confusion at how we'd been overwhelmed and where such a massive horde had come from. Anger that we'd become so complacent. Sorrow at the loss of my friends, all in suits without support skeletons. There was another wave of panic in there at some point, screaming and thrashing and crying. I think I blacked out for a little while. It's hard to say.

It's the lack of a decision that's gnawing on me. Every survivor knows that there might come a time when they have to decide between infection and a bullet. That choice has been taken from me. All I can do is lie here and listen to my new friends try desperately to eat me alive. It turns out, if the school's big enough, even toothless piranhas can gum you to death.

Huh, I like that. It's witty. I wish I could tell it to somebody.

Zombie Plague

By Spencer Carvalho

Taylor and Jack lived in the house that they inherited from their parents. Their dad passed away in a tragic jetpack testing accident. Their mom was killed by dolphins on vacation. The mom was on vacation, not the dolphins.

Bruce was visiting them. Jack met Bruce at a charity zombie walk. It was a charity walk to raise cancer awareness. Apparently there were still a few people who never heard of cancer. Jack told Bruce that he had a sister but didn't really describe her. When Bruce first met Taylor their eyes locked for a second. He saw a beautiful woman wearing a shirt with a dragon fighting a unicorn. The coolest part was that the unicorn was winning. He was instantly smitten.

"I just got Left 4 Dead 3," said Jack. "This is the best zombie killing game ever made."

"I call the chainsaw," said Taylor.

They headed into the living room for game time. Had they been paying attention to the television they would have heard the newsman talking about some strange epidemic with undead people walking around.

"Apparently we have received reports of people previously thought to be dead showing signs of movement. We have reports that this is not just a local situation, it... "

The game turned on.

They played video games until exhaustion stopped them. Bruce was the first one up and he sluggishly made his way to the bathroom. As he was urinating he noticed something strange out the window. Jack's neighbour, Dorothy Prescott, was wandering around her yard. It distracted him so much that he made a mess.

"Ah crap," said Bruce.

He grabbed a towel and cleaned up. "Hey, the old lady next door is wandering around," said Bruce leaving the bathroom.

"Oh yeah, she's senile," said Jack. "She sometimes does strange things. Hey, the power must have gone out last night. My digital clock is flashing."

"Is the beer okay?" asked Taylor.

"Probably," said Bruce. "Good priorities."

Jack walked over to the TV and turned it on. They froze when they saw news footage of a deserted city street. The newsman was heard speaking off screen.

"... is widespread. It seems to be happening all over America. There is no explanation yet why this is happening but it seems that the dead are coming back to life and eating any living thing that they find. Please be advised to avoid these creatures at all costs. Many places that are affected by this situation are reporting loss of power; so if you are able to view this, please inform others. We will update you as more information comes in."

They had all wondered what it would be like to go through a zombie apocalypse. Ever since they were little and saw their first zombie movie. They had envisioned scenarios and survival tactics. Taylor and Jack had many conversations about the best way to decapitate a zombie whilst growing up.

"I know that he didn't say zombie but... that sure seems like a zombie thing," said Jack.

"Sure seems that way," said Taylor.

"This is real?" asked Bruce. "This can't be real, right? On the news it said something about loss of power but we still have power so that means this area is safe?"

"Actually we have a solar panel on the roof," said Jack. "The power must have gone out during the night after we went to sleep and then when it was light outside we got the power back on. That's why my digital clock was flashing."

"Good job going green," said Bruce.

"So we'll have power until it gets dark," said Jack.

"Oh!" said Taylor. "Weapons! We need weapons."

Taylor got up and left and they followed her down to the basement. They followed Taylor to her dad's rifle cabinet. They stared for a few seconds at the four weapons inside.

"This is perfect," said Bruce.

"Actually no," said Jack. "The rifle on the right is out of bullets and the shot gun on the left is broken so only two of the guns work. Have any of you guys ever fired a gun before?"

"Only bb guns," said Taylor.

"I've gone skeet shooting before," said Bruce. "I've also used double-barrel shotguns before."

Jack opened the case and handed Bruce the double-barrel shotgun.

"Whoa, hold on a second," said Taylor. "Maybe you guys forgot about last night but I by far had the highest score on the video game."

"That was a video game," said Jack.

"Yeah, a zombie shooting video game," said Taylor. "Given the circumstances it's more like a simulation than a game. I might even be the most qualified person here."

"I'm not giving you a gun because you're good at a video game," said Jack. "Bruce is good at driving games and we all know how much he sucks at actual driving."

"I'm a great driver," said Bruce. "It's everyone else that sucks."

"Remember the ducks?" asked Jack.

Bruce stared off into space as memories of the tragic duck massacre rushed back.

"Poor duckies," said Bruce.

Jack opened up the lower part of the cabinet and handed out ammo. Bruce loaded his double barrel shotgun and put some spare shells in his pocket. Jack put a bullet in the chamber of his rifle and checked the safety.

"What am I supposed to do?" asked Taylor. "I've seen what happens to people without weapons in zombie movies."

"There are other things you can use as weapons," said Jack. "There's a lot of stuff in the garage."

They made their way up to the garage. Taylor looked around and quickly found a baseball bat but continued looking for something better.

"Yes!" yelled Taylor.

She reached down over a pile of boxes. Jack and Bruce looked over to see what she was grabbing. Taylor pulled what she wanted out and turned around holding the object of her desire high above her head with both hands. The other two guys just stood in quiet amazement and marvelled at Taylor's wonderful discovery. Jack had completely forgotten about the chainsaw.

"Groovy," said Taylor.

"Do you want to trade?" asked Bruce.

"No way. You can keep your boomstick. I've just become a

killing machine."

Bruce watched Taylor swing around the chainsaw and turned to Jack.

"Your sister is perfection," said Bruce.

Jack sighed.

"We should check on the neighbours," said Jack.

They were not going to miss the chance to kill some zombies. This was the moment they had been waiting for. Jack hit the switch for the garage door.

Once outside they looked down at the house of Jack's closest neighbours, the Prescotts. They saw the elderly Dorothy Prescott staggering around the yard. She was unaware of their presence.

"So um, I have a question," said Taylor. "Is she a zombie or senile because I don't want to kill an innocent old lady?"

"Let me check," said Jack. "Hello! Mrs. Prescott! Excuse me ma'am, are you a zombie?"

Dorothy looked up towards the guys. She had bloodstains around her mouth. She slowly started making her way towards them with a hungry look.

"She's a zombie!" said Jack. "It's okay to kill the old lady."

Dorothy continued toward them. They just stared at her. Jack raised his rifle and aimed it at her. He remembered how she always gave out regular sized candy bars at Halloween instead of the tiny fun-size bars that weren't fun at all.

"I can't kill her," said Jack. "She was always really nice to me."

"Fine," said Taylor. "I'll do it. The old bag used to call me a harlot."

Taylor pulled the ripcord. Nothing happened. She tried it again and nothing happened.

"I think the chainsaw is broken," said Taylor.

Jack looked at the chainsaw for a few seconds.

"Oh!" said Jack. "It's probably out of gas. There's a tank in the garage."

Taylor ran towards the garage. The zombie old lady slowly continued her way towards them.

"Hurry up!" said Bruce.

The zombie old lady was now only a few feet from them. Bruce raised his weapon and aimed it at the zombie old lady. He was getting ready to fire when Taylor ran past them and hit the zombie old lady in the head with a baseball bat. The first hit knocked her to the ground. Taylor continued her attack. The others backed away to avoid splatter. Taylor continued until the zombie old lady stopped moving. Taylor stood over the zombie corpse. She didn't even notice the mess that covered her shirt.

"She's so badass," said Bruce.

Jack sighed.

Jack and Bruce moved in closer to better see the zombie corpse.

"You're sure she was a zombie right?" asked Taylor.

"I sure hope so," said Jack.

Taylor walked back to the garage and returned with the chainsaw.

"It's fuelled up," said Taylor.

They moved on to the house. They stopped at the bottom of the steps leading up to the doorway. The door was shut.

"Should we knock?" asked Bruce.

Bruce walked up three steps to the door and knocked. He pushed the button for the doorbell but there was no sound. He then remembered that the power was out for all homes without a solar panel. He looked back at the guys below and smiled at his foolishness. He waited a few seconds and then knocked again.

"At least we now know what kind of zombies we're dealing with," said Jack. "If they were the fast zombies then things would be tough but with the slow ones you could probably take them out pretty easy."

"Yeah, hope so," said Bruce. "There might be people inside. I'm going to break in."

"How are you going to do that?" asked Jack.

Bruce took the handle of his double barrel shotgun and knocked the doorknob off. The door creaked open a few inches.

"So much for the illusion of security," said Taylor. "Hey Jack, you said that they're slow because Dorothy was slow but she was slow when she was alive too."

Bruce slowly started pushing open the door with his double barrel shotgun.

"So?" asked Jack.

"Well," said Taylor. "Why would she become faster after turning?"

A zombie ran out the door into Bruce knocking him to the ground and landing on top of him. It started trying to bite at Bruce's face but the shotgun was keeping its head back. Bruce tried pushing it off but it was too heavy.

"Help!" screamed Bruce.

Taylor started up the chainsaw and moved toward the zombie. She tried to angle the chainsaw in a way that she could kill it without killing Bruce but they were too close together. Jack ran up and kicked the zombie off Bruce. The zombie, quick as a snake, leapt to its feet before Jack shot it in the chest knocking it onto its back. Bruce got to his feet and pointed his gun at the zombie who was still moving. Taylor ran between them with the chainsaw held high above her head and brought it down on the zombie's neck. Blood and decayed flesh flew up into the air. Taylor was getting really messy. After a minute of chainsawing Taylor backed away from the mess on the floor. Bruce turned to Taylor.

"You are perfection," said Bruce.

Taylor smiled.

"Oh, really," said Taylor. "Aren't you sweet? I really hope you survive this zombie apocalypse."

"Me too," said Bruce.

Jack sighed. He then reloaded his rifle and walked up the stairs to the doorway. He had the weapon ready to fire. He yelled into the house.

"Is there anyone alive in here?"

There was only silence. They searched the house but couldn't find anyone.

"Oh my God," said Taylor.

"What?" asked Jack.

Jack and Bruce raised their weapons.

"Our neighbours were literally zombies, right?" asked Taylor.

"Yes," said Jack.

Taylor started getting excited.

"So that means that they were turned into zombies by another zombie that bit them," said Taylor. "When it bit them it probably ate some of them. Get it?"

Taylor smiled.

"Are you serious?" asked Jack.

"What?" asked Bruce.

"Zombies ate my neighbours," said Taylor. "Zombies literally ate my neighbours."

Jack sighed.

"You're insane," said Jack.

"Oh, like the video game," said Bruce. "I loved that game."

Bruce and Taylor laughed. Jack sighed again.

"You're both insane," said Jack.

They grabbed some supplies and went back to their house. They gathered in the kitchen area. Jack put the cold items in the refrigerator. Taylor put her bloody chainsaw up on the counter.

"Come on," said Jack.

"Oh, sorry," said Taylor.

She moved the bloody chainsaw to the sink.

"So what do we do now?" asked Taylor.

"We could go to S Mart for supplies," said Bruce. "Shop smart, shop S Mart."

"No, we're not going there," said Jack. "It's a high population area so there are probably a lot of zombies there and if there are people around then they might be desperate or crazy. People in zombie movies usually get crazy and violent pretty quickly."

"Do you have a plan?" asked Taylor.

"Yeah, we do the smart thing," said Jack. "In all the zombie movies we've seen over the years people always get killed off by doing stupid things. We will do the one thing that they never try. We'll wait it out."

Jack looked to see their reaction. They said nothing.

"It makes sense right?" asked Jack. "Zombies decay so if we stay safe for a while eventually they'll be so decrepit that we could speed walk past them. We have water and enough food to last us several days. If our food supply runs out we can always go door to door and raid the empty houses. Let's not try to hole up at a mall or make our way to an island or any of that dumb stuff. Let's just stay here for a while."

They looked at each other to see if anyone was going to disagree with this plan. They all nodded in agreement.

"What about me?" asked Bruce.

"You can stay in my room," said Taylor.

Bruce smiled while Jack sighed again.

"Well, okay," said Jack. "So we have a plan."

"Uh, this might be weird," said Bruce. "But while we have power, do any of you want to play some more Left 4 Dead 3?"

"I call the chainsaw," said Taylor.

I, Zombie

A Voice in My Head

By Scott Woodward

This is how it begins. A voice jars me into existence.

"Awake." The voice echoes in my head, displacing the void. Its urgency surges through my limbs, compelling my body to obey.

I try to sit up, but my head crashes into the ceiling. I feel all around myself, I'm trapped in an oblong box. The voice commands me to lash out with my feet, and I kick against the square freezer door until it wrenches from its hinges and clatters to the tile floor. I pull myself free and drop to the floor.

A young woman, blonde hair gathered into a ponytail that streams behind her, rushes into the room and gapes at me. I would spare her, but the voice commands otherwise. I lunge forward and am on her, hands clasped around her slender neck and throttling, before she can scream. I lift her body off the ground by her delicate neck and feel repeated blows against my shins as her legs thrash in protest. Afterwards, when she hangs limp in my arms, the voice instructs me to hide her body in the very freezer that I so recently occupied.

I follow the directives in my head until I find my uniform, blood-stained and neatly folded in a box labelled 'Doe, J.' It takes longer than anticipated to dress, and the voice in my head grows impatient. I finally finish and lurch to the elevator, jabbing the button repeatedly until the doors open and I stagger inside. Mercifully, it is devoid of other occupants.

***

The lift whirs upward from the purgatory of the morgue and bounces to a stop on the top floor of the building. The doors rattle open, and I'm greeted by a dimly lit corridor and the distant hum of mechanical ventilators and an occasional

62

geriatric cough. The air smells of bleach and artificial pine, both of which fail to mask the underlying odour of rot and corruption, scents I know well.

I gaze at the placards on the wall, guiding visitors, but cannot decipher the words. The voice commands me to turn right. I stagger down the hall toward the nurses' station on legs that do not seem to be my own.

Even at this hour, it is occupied by a middle-aged woman with auburn hair corralled into a bun and reading glasses dangling from a silver chain looped around her neck. She had been dozing and jerks awake at my presence, eyes bulging as she stares at my face, fixating on the patches of skull visible through my parchment-like skin. No doubt, she wonders if she's still dreaming and if her dream has taken some unsanctioned detour toward nightmare.

Before she can scream, I lunge forward and grasp her head between my hands, slamming it onto the wooden desktop with enough force to crack its wooden surface as well as her skull. The voice forces me to do this repeatedly until her head is mush between my hands. "Hurry," the voice commands.

I stagger down the corridor, passing numerous doors until I halt in front of room 619. From inside, I hear the laboured mechanical breathing of a ventilator.

I thrust the door open and lurch through the doorway. My shadow stretches across the room to caress a pallid face I recognize despite the intervening decades. As if awakened by the weight of my gaze, the man's eyes flutter open, and the ventilator hiccups as he gasps in surprise. He tries to speak, but his words are swallowed by the plastic tube taped into his mouth.

The voice commands and I obey. I bend down and lift him from the bed. His hospital gown is clammy with sweat, and he squirms in my arms, but he is far removed from his prime and unable to resist. The array of umbilical cords connected to his body pull free and the machine by his bed begins to beep in distress. I ignore these distractions and stagger toward the window. His struggles grow frantic as we approach the window, his head whipping back and forth in mute protest. The voice leaves me no option. I hurl his body through the window, shattering the glass and sending him plummeting downward to burst apart on the pavement below.

I hear distant screams rising from the parking lot and, from within my own skull, laughing.

**

It is broad daylight as I reel along a sidewalk washed white by sunlight. The birds chattering in the trees lining the walkway grow silent as I draw near and then take flight, heralding my approach. Ahead, loom two sliding glass doors, and I watch myself lurch unevenly toward them, the tarnished iron cross on my chest glinting in their mirrored glass.

The doors slide open at my approach, and I stagger into the shadowed interior of the building. I hear a hiss as the doors shut, and the sudden absence of sound makes it seem as if I'm underwater. The light filters through the tinted glass, casting dappled shadows across the tiled floor. I hear voices laughing and speaking in a language I cannot understand. A small dog's yapping echoes down the corridor.

"Proceed," the voice commands.

I try to resist and, for a time, I'm successful. But her will dwarfs mine, and I'm soon propelled forward, boots clomping across the polished tile floor. I can no more resist her commands than a rook can resist the hand that sends it sliding across a chessboard.

Everyone is gathered in a common area, seated on the array of sofas and overstuffed chairs in the room. Several women and one man are bound to wheelchairs positioned adjacent to the couches. Staff members, dressed in white uniforms, stand in proximity to their elderly charges or lean against the walls, wishing they were elsewhere. All of the assembled group are watching a young woman as she takes the dog she holds from one elderly resident to the next, allowing them to pet the dog or give it a treat.

The dog, some kind of terrier with fur the colour of day-old snow, is the first to notice my arrival. It struggles in its owner's arms, staring at me, a low growl rumbling in its chest. Its owner follows the dog's gaze until her eyes, magnified behind rectangular lenses, widen in shock. She gasps and the dog squirms free of her arms, dropping to the floor, where it lands in an ungainly manner with splayed legs. It barks at me several times and then bolts down the hall, chased by its owner.

Other heads turn toward me and a murmur ripples through the gathering. A beast of a man dressed in the uniform of a security guard approaches me but then hesitates as he stares at my rotting flesh wrapped in a field grey uniform. He speaks to me, but I cannot understand his words as the voice chooses not to translate. Although he towers above me and outweighs my desiccated body by more than a hundred pounds, it makes no difference.

"Now," the voice commands as the guard darts forward, arms outstretched to apprehend me.

I swat his grasping arms aside and seize his head with my hands. His eyes bulge in surprise; he is unaccustomed to being physically dominated. The voice tells me to squeeze, and I do so until his shrieks end with sound of his skull cracking like brittle ice.

I lay his body aside and turn toward an old man in a wheelchair, abandoned to his fate by the panicked staff. He too looks familiar. I subtract decades of hard living and add a flamethrower and confirm his identity, at least to myself. The witch knew it all along. Why else was I here?

"Now," she commands.

I stagger forward. The frail shell of my former comrade, a man once so virile and hard we had nicknamed him 'Oak,' waves his skeletal arms and mouths incoherent pleas as if these might stave off his impending doom. I pluck my former comrade from the confines of his wheelchair and embrace him to my chest, his legs dangling limply above the floor. His hoarse screams fill my head as I begin to squeeze, but the voice inside me, driving me onward, is louder still. I crush him to my chest until I feel his sternum and ribs shatter and the blood filling his mouth spatters on my tunic.

***

"Awake."

I find myself in the back of a van, lying among assorted tools and scraps of wood like something found in a refuse pile. Waning afternoon light trickles through the tinted rear windows and illuminates the tattered pants of my uniform.

The rear doors of the van are yanked open with a metallic screech. A young woman, perhaps the same age I was before I perished in that cursed city on the Volga, stands before me, jiggling from foot to foot. Dressed in denim pants and a black leather jacket that would not look out of place on an agent of the Gestapo, she feigns a smirk, but this veneer falters as I crawl toward her. Whatever she may be elsewhere, here she is a scared teenage driver and nothing more.

She backpedals from the van's doors as I pull myself from its confines to stand at last upon terra firma. The girl takes a hesitant step toward me and points to a two-storey house to my left.

"Go," the voice in my head orders. I lurch forward, nearly tripping over a curb, and stagger across the manicured lawn. I can hear children giggling and music drifting across the lawn from the backyard. Periodically, I hear the sound of something papery and firm being whacked by a plastic stick or bat.

The voice pushes me onward and steers me toward a wooden gate at the side of the house. Although I hear laughter and that intermittent thwacking sound, I see no one. I fumble with the metal latch and then push through the gates and into the side yard. As I pass two air conditioning units – squat, corroded beasts perched on steel platforms a foot above the ground – I detect movement out of the corner of my eye.

A boy, maybe three or four, with a mop of blond hair that shimmers in the late afternoon sunlight, is playing with metal cars in the gravel near the air conditioners. The slender white stick of a lollypop handle extends from his juice-stained lips. His eyes bulge at the sight of me, but he smiles and stretches a diminutive arm upward, offering me one of his toys. I would smile if only I could.

"Kill the whelp," the voice orders. But this time, she has made a mistake. The meaning of the word 'whelp' is unclear, and I am not compelled to obey. I stagger forward toward the main host of the party before she can rephrase her command. I hear her fuming in my head, promising further torment, but her threats ring hollow. What could she do to me that would be worse than what she has already done?

I round the corner of the house and lurch to a stop, swaying in the breeze that blows off the Potomac River. A group of middle school girls, wearing softball uniforms, surround a cardboard giraffe suspended from a branch of the birch tree looming above the house. One girl, in the centre of the circle formed by her teammates, has a kerchief tied around her eyes and is swinging a plastic bat at the giraffe. I can hear the whoosh of the bat as it cleaves a path through the autumn air.

The adults are gathered around a picnic table covered in a plastic cloth depicting animated princesses and piled high with brightly-wrapped boxes. Most are young mothers fixated on their daughters across the lawn or chatting amiably, but I see an older woman, a grandmother, wrapped in a shawl who is serving a piece of cake that appears to be mostly frosting to a toddler perched at the table.

The sliding glass door to my left grates open, and an old man, whose face I would know anywhere, tentatively steps through the door clutching the frame for support. Behind him, carrying two glasses filled with lemonade, is a middle-aged man, lean and angular. His brown hair is streaked with grey, and he reminds me of my own father. The grandfather reaches the picnic table and smiles at his wife, as if that were a major accomplishment.

The sound of glass shattering on the patio bricks seizes my attention. The father is staring at me, trembling. His hands that until recently were securely clasped around glasses, grasp at empty air.

The others turn to look; I hear gasps and a curse uttered in my own language. Mercifully, the girls are still caught up in their game and have not noticed me, an unwelcome intruder into the lives of others.

"Now," the voice commands. I try to resist, but my body moves forward of its own accord.

The father recovers his wits and takes a hesitant step toward me, blocking my path.

"Who... " he starts to ask, but before he can finish, my left arm lashes out and strikes his neck with the force of a two-by-four. His body catapults sideways and crashes through the sliding glass doors to lie sprawled on the beige carpet. Shards of glass strewn across his clothing gleam in the fading light.

Shouts and screams envelop me, but my puppeteer is undeterred. She advances me toward the stooped grandfather, who is clutching the table with one hand and motioning his wife to flee with the other. I see several women dart across the lawn toward their daughters.

One mother, tears streaming from her eyes and wielding a butcher's knife still coated in frosting, lunges forward and drives the knife into my chest to its wooden handle. I appreciate her audacity, but my controller does not. My hands grasp her head, her hair spilling between my fingers, and twist with such force that I hear the vertebrae in her neck splinter.

I lurch forward on a path of destruction. My arms flail and knock fleeing guests aside as I grasp the collar of the fleeing grandfather and yank him backwards off his feet and into my arms, which encircle his chest and squeeze. I stare down at his pallid face, the scar from a bullet still visible on his right cheek bone after all these decades. I squeeze until his sternum collapses and his eyes roll back into his head, revealing whites yellowed by age and nicotine. I squeeze until she finally permits me to stop.

"Papa?" A small voice asks behind me. I turn to find the pre-schooler I had left playing with his toy cars standing behind me.

"Kill the child," the voice commands. Her will drags my legs forward until I loom over him, my shadow enveloping his diminutive body. I wonder whose child he is, and if I have already killed his parents.

He still clutches toy cars in hands that are barely large enough to hold them. I scream, if only in my mind, as my arm stretches above my head and then hurtles downward to shatter his fragile skull and send his baby-fresh body rebounding off the patio bricks.

The voice makes me stand, rigid as fence post, and watch as blood and brain tissue seep from his splintered skull. I watch as his wispy angel hair becomes matted and dark with blood. I watch until my soul withers under the weight of my crimes. I watch until she finally releases me.

I stagger back the way I came, through the side gate and lurch across the lawn toward the waiting van. In the

8

distance I hear sirens and more closely, screams and shouts. The witch's daughter is standing by the van's back doors. Exhaust pluming from its tailpipe billows around her body, making her appear like a conjurer's assistant.

***

Such was our haste in fleeing that the witch neglects to relinquish me to the void. I stare at the bone-coloured ceiling of the van whilst my corpse rolls back-and-forth as the witch's daughter sends the vehicle careening around corners and jostling over potholes as we drive through the deepening gloom. The wooden knife handle still protrudes from the centre of my chest like a vampire's stake.

Much later the van slows, and I hear gravel bouncing along the undercarriage and then the sound of some vast door grinding open. The vehicle creeps forward into some warehouse, the hitching sound of its engine echoing hollowly around us. Then the door rumbles shut behind us, and the girl kills the engine. I hear her throw open the driver's door and then the sound of her boots clomping along concrete toward the back of the van.

She throws the doors open and grasps my ankles, careful not to touch any of the rotting flesh beneath my socks. She strains as she pulls my corpse toward the van doors, but the witch's daughter has made a mistake. Unaware that I remain sentient, she has carelessly let herself get within reach. My arm lashes out, and the fingers of my hand encircle the pale flesh of her neck.

Her eyes widen in shock, and a froth of saliva seeps from her gaping mouth to coat a purple-hued lip. Never did she imagine perishing at the hands of her mother's slave. I know I have only seconds before the witch herself becomes aware of my treason. I dash the girl's head against the side of the van with a metallic clang like the toll of some infernal bell.

A howl of grief echoes through my head followed by silence.

***

The warehouse is surrounded. The sounds of their fists pounding against the corrugated steel door echo throughout the building's vacant interior. I peer through a dust-coated window and see scores of automatons shambling through the night. Most are empty-handed, arms stretching forward as they lurch unevenly toward the warehouse to join the host assembling at the door.

Several of the approaching corpses carry plastic jerry cans with missing lids and I watch as liquid sloshes and spills out of these containers with each lumbering step. The witch has removed the caps, knowing her minions lack the dexterity to do so themselves. I see another of my kind hanging well back from the others and holding a burning flare in its hand, which illuminates the flesh sloughing from its skull.

A phalanx of corpses, each armed with a pickaxe, escort a woman dressed in a claret sarafan, her head wrapped in scarf the colour of a winter sky. The witch has come herself to witness my immolation.

I cast my eyes about the interior of the warehouse searching amidst the broken glass, pools of water, and piles of debris strewn across the concrete floor for a weapon. I hear the sound of metal scraping concrete and see the pointed blade of pickaxe protrude into the warehouse from underneath the cargo door as one of her minions tries to pry the door upward. They will succeed eventually if I do nothing and I must do so before the witch regains control!

I move as quickly as my rotting legs will permit to the driver's side door of the van, which is still ajar. I reach inside and pull the emergency brake lever. The van shifts only slightly backwards toward the cargo door and then settles. I'm still trying to think, but am out of habit, when I notice a black box the size of a packet of cigarettes clipped to the van's visor. The witch's daughter had not exited the vehicle until we had already entered the warehouse and I had heard the cargo door rumble open upon our approach. I fumble at the device until a finger depresses a round button in its centre and I hear the door grind upwards, its chain squeaking in protest as it lifts the door.

I stagger to the front of the van, place both hands on its faded white hood, and push. The van begins to roll backwards. Slowly at first, but then it gains momentum as if relishing the prospect of crushing the horde congregated at the loading bay door, which is now more than halfway open.

The loading bay door rumbles completely open, exposing a throng of desiccated corpses, dressed in tattered uniforms that surge forward in unison. They do not get far. The first few members of the procession have only just entered the warehouse when the five thousand pound cargo van rolls into them, smashing their bodies backward with a metallic crunch that echoes off the concrete walls of the warehouse. One of the zombies, who carries a plastic jerry, is crushed under the vehicle, and the pungent odour of gasoline wafts through the warehouse as the container spills across the loading dock.

I stagger forward in the van's wake. The vehicle has halted atop a pile of broken but squirming corpses. I hear a hiss of rage and see the witch, still surrounded by her praetorian guard, surveying the carnage. The van has bought me time, but there are still too many, and I remain unarmed.

I spot a five-gallon plastic container lying on its side and grasp it in my hand. It still has maybe a gallon of petrol left inside. I raise it above my head and tilt it until the gasoline cascades down my head and shoulders, drenching my uniform; the first baptism of my undeath.

One of her servants, arms outstretched and groaning in anticipation, stalks toward me. With the van blocking most of the loading bay, the remaining zombies are forced to proceed single file on either side of the van. Despite this, it's only a matter of minutes until I'm surrounded.

I shove the approaching zombie before it can embrace me

and it staggers backwards into another following too closely behind it. I continue moving forward and reach the front of the van. I see the witch and her bodyguards standing apart from the fray, waiting no doubt for me to be subdued. Closer, I see the torchbearer still wielding the flare, which blazes with red flame and emits a cloud of sparks and grey smoke.

I push past the two zombies blocking my path and break free of the confines of the warehouse. The witch, sensing my plan, sends her guard surging toward me, pickaxes raised in silent menace. But I am closer to the torchbearer and reach him before they can stop me. I grasp his upraised arm in both my hands and pull the sparking flare toward my gasoline-soaked body.

My tunic ignites with an acrid stench, and my vision is clouded by plumes of yellow and orange flame. I embrace the torchbearer setting him ablaze before turning toward the advancing guards who are now swinging their pickaxes wildly in a futile effort to prevent me from reaching them. I am a walking Roman candle and, for the first time, an instrument of my own vengeance.

The gravel parking lot is lit by the light of burning corpses, all of which stagger or crawl toward me. They are unrelenting, but they are too few and too slow to save the witch who recoils from my advance, her head shaking in disbelief.

This is how it ends, with the witch afire and shrieking. No commands fill my head, only gibbering agony. And then, the silence of the void.

The End of All Flesh on Mango Street

By Alex H Leclerc

My jaw dropped to the floor. Literally.

"Argh gurgh," I exclaimed. Damn flesh-eating disease.

I was surprised, but I saw it coming. The flesh-eating plague attacked my mouth first. It was just a matter of time for the ligaments to give out.

But expressing myself had just become troublesome.

I bent to pick up my chin and lower teeth. I took a step to keep my balance, and kicked them away. "Herk," I swore. I bent again, took another step to keep from faceplanting on my own teeth. Kicked my jaw again. "Heeerk!"

I finally grabbed my jawbone off the floor and went to the bathroom to get a good look in the mirror. A tongue is impressively long without a jaw. I could lick my chest. The word 'lollygagging' sprang to my mind for some reason.

I looked grisly, so I tried to fit my jaw back in. With my cheeks eaten away by the disease, it was child's play to jimmy it into place. It wouldn't stay put, though.

So I duct-taped it. From my chin around to the top of my skull, three times. *At least, I still have my permanent smile*, I thought.

I went down the rusting fire escape stairs to the deserted, litter-covered street for my morning walk. Well, it was more of a shamble at that point. I went down Mango Street and took a left along the canal. It was nicer there. It was good for my soul to escape the grey city and get a little dose of nature.

Also there were fewer corpses there than on the roads. Though there was the occasional bloated body floating downriver. *At least I won't have to step over those*, I thought. *Or dodge their ankle bites.*

I threaded my way across the alley. I had to navigate between trash bags spilling their guts, piles of bricks, broken glass, and a dead cat to reach the riverside.

The unkempt grass was knee high and clumps of wildflowers grew through the cracks in the bike path. The brown waters of the canal churned with its green and white grocery bags swirling in the eddies. There were the cries of crows and ravens, the smell of wet trash, the grey trees, the yellow sky. I felt the tepid wind against my face, blowing grit in my eyes and teeth, tasting like burnt rubber.

Morning walks... er, shambles, are so energizing.

I walked to the boat landing where I had set a couple of traps. It was a prime watering hole with easy access to the water for the few animals still untouched by the plague. I guess trapping was more trouble than looting a corner store, but it was also safer. No human bands with weapons. No hordes. No ankle biters.

I checked my traps. Nothing. Though all the collars I had set up had been triggered. I swore a phlegmy curse. My fingers were getting too clumsy for the fine knots. *My boyscout days are over*, I thought.

I took an hour to set the collars back up. I was setting the third one when it hit me.

Without a working jaw, how am I supposed to eat?

I ripped the trap apart, growling like an asthmatic pug, and threw it in the canal.

My shoulder popped out of its socket and my arm fell to my side, limp as a slice of raw bacon.

I stared at it. Glowered at it.

After some cursing and dirt kicking, I slumped down. The water cascaded over the collapsed pedestrian bridge. Flowering shrubs bloomed among the cement slabs and twisting metal railings. Tears were running down my face and on my teeth. I tasted salt.

"Get a grip, you big baby," I mumbled through my duct-taped jaw.

I wiped my face on my sleeve. On the retaining wall across the water, the words 'house of cards' were spray painted in black over the red-and-blue poster of the last government. *When the cards have toppled*, I thought, *where is the house?*

I lay down in the sun and closed my eyes.

Apologies to Lazarus

By E.F. Schraeder

The damp, cool basement air didn't bother Rus as he lumbered toward the weekly weigh-in he required of this small, odd family. Nor did the sour, pungent stench sting his nostrils as it once had. He'd grown used to these faint harbingers of their unholy weekly communions.

Rus took a laboured step onto the scale, eyed it, and stepped off. "I'm Rus and I've got eating problems," he said, best as his rotted jawbone allowed.

Discordant voices greeted him with varying abilities of speech control.

"Hi!"

"Ah-h."

"Rus."

"Br-a-ains!"

"Who said 'brains'?" Rus blurted, spittle dripped from his lower lip. He angrily wiped it with the hem of his shirtsleeve, taking a bit of grey lip along with the effort. "Damn!" he cried, pressing the oozing lip until it hastened closed.

"Not funny," Rus wagged a finger at the crowded room. He stared at them, searching for a tell that didn't come.

Just silence. A snicker. Then the wet sound of a blown nose. *Rory.*

Rus stared at the six rows of metal folding chairs. Into the chairs were strewn bodies. Bodies of those he'd once loved, with their joints swung at unnatural angles. Another dozen or so bodies lined the back wall around the table, where they dipped their hands into a punchbowl and fed themselves mouthfuls of something that looked like a thick, sloppy red

77

soup.

Rus shivered, then wobbled onto the scale.

"Still 150," Rus said. He slashed a mark into the broad black book on the podium. "Who's next?"

No one volunteered. But someone belched, sending a waft of foul, dead breath, sour and thick, over the bobbing heads in the tan metal chairs. A few in attendance groaned as the familiar smell of decay drifted nearby.

Rus didn't react except for a scowl and nostril flare. He pursed his lips and sent his eyes from the scale to the untidy crowd. He stood beside the scale, tapped the spot on his wrist where a watch would be, had he an appointment for anything other than the reaper. His wan face, impatient. "This keeps us right, now," Rus said. It was best to keep sentences short. "Weight tracks decay," he added.

"And intake," someone sniggered in the back.

Rus nodded and stroked his chin where a rough beard once grew. Skin sloughed in his hands that he wiped onto his trousers. How he hated the rancid stink of himself. No matter how often he changed clothes, he could only afford to wash the fetid skin so much without incurring more rot. The more bodies he infected, the worse the decomposition progressed. *Why didn't they understand? The hunger,* he answered. *The hunger was that bad.*

"Follow the diet. Follow the diet." A woman's voice came from the middle of the room in a scolding tone.

One of my sisters. Wenches! Their damn fault! They could never keep from the food, dead or alive.

"Ingesting flesh hastens rot. Restraint purifies," Rus said. Anger turned to rage inside the rotten coils of his black, infested intestines. He cursed the day he woke up like this, and the bastards that brought him to it, sisters included.

***

Putrid, stale air hung in the tomb with the kind of stench that would choke the living, but it didn't bother Rus. Eyes opened, squinting in the dark. He couldn't discern anything and remained motionless, trying to remember how he'd arrived, but it was a thick blur.

Moving his mouth, he noticed a sticky cloth wrapped around his face. *What old ritual was this?* Probably his sister Mary's doing. *One of her damned superstitions.*

Rus moved a hand to the face and began to unwrap himself. "Like a mummy," he said, half laughing. His skin stuck, stinging as he peeled off strips with the gauzy material. "Ow," he yelled.

He stopped, leaving a wide, white shred of fabric dangling over one eye. "That's enough," he said. He yanked the last piece off, tearing the fabric away from his oozing skin.

He pressed the loose bits from his torn face, checking for bleeding. The patches were wet. He tossed the face wrap to the ground. It looked like a shroud. *What the hell?*

Rus felt a strange, hollow burning in the stomach and remembered being sick, sleeping for days at his dear sister Mary's house on Bethany Drive. He rubbed his belly, noticed the skin so clammy and cool, a little bloated. He pressed harder. Fluid shot from his mouth. "Ugh!" he cried.

Then only a deep-seated pain remained, like an impossible aching hunger. The taste of bile stung his throat.

Rus inhaled, sucking in damp air. A nasty rattle erupted in a raspy cough, loosening something in his chest. He swallowed, though the film in his mouth burned like bile. Then a faint, gnawing nausea swelled.

"Where am I?" Rus pushed himself up, leaning on the wall with one hand. Now standing, his head felt as if it spun. He couldn't focus his eyes on anything as the room whirled, so he gripped the wall.

His legs were definitely weak, giving out, so he moved slowly. Inch by inch, Rus lowered himself back down to the ground. "Oh, you've got to be kidding me," he said into the empty dark. "Whole lot of nothing here."

Rus felt along his pant leg, searching for his phone, but he didn't have any pockets. Only white linen pants, practically in shreds. "Did I get mugged or what? Who snaked my pants?" The linen was so frail that it tore in his fingers.

"Mary?" Rus called, hoping his sisters hadn't been dumped there too. "Martha?"

No answer came. The cool, clammy air kept its peace in the constant dark.

"Anyone?" his voice pleading. The knot of bile hardened in his throat. He choked it back again.

"Damn. What's with these funky clothes?" He pulled at the linens, tugging them off his arms in shreds. "Cheap-ass hospital pajamas. Feel like paper."

Rus didn't remember going to the hospital, but he was sick enough that maybe he'd lost consciousness for a few days. Or blacked out. He'd taken plenty of pain killers that could've knocked him out.

Who brought me here? Wherever here was.

Now bare chested, the cold became numbing. Rus's arms and torso tingled then went dead. "Shit." He fingered the rags, hoping there'd be a way he could have something to cover himself, but it was hopeless. Even in the blackness he could tell his skin was already turning bluish-grey in the cold. Now he knew to leave his pants alone no matter what condition they were in. It was better than freezing to death.

"Whoever the hell stuck me down here is gonna pay for this. This is crap!" An even, steady anger built. He chuckled.

80

"Well, rage warms me up at least."

Rus felt a painful gurgle in his stomach and applied the pressure of his hand. It seemed to help. He realized that pain was actually hunger, deeper than any he'd known. Made sense. He wouldn't have been eating if he'd been unconscious.

"Hungry," he growled. "A little food would be nice!" he yelled to no one.

A strange, sour taste filled his mouth, accompanied by thick coating on his tongue. He gagged a few times, hoping the taste would clear out if he spit. He scraped his teeth against his tongue and sent the spittle soaring. He recoiled, horrified to see a spray of bloody mucous beside on the ground. "Maybe I'm not quite well yet," he said. He coughed and choked up another chunk.

"Can't see," Rus mumbled, fumbling again at the wall. His voice raised along with a deep, visceral frustration.

"Too dark," he yelled. Rus tried again to press himself up along the wall and noticed the cold matching the cold of his own hand. He fingered the wall, hoping for a light switch, but found nothing.

"Nothing." He slapped and pounded his body against the wall as his anger pitched. "What kind of monster would dump a sick man in a dungeon like this?" he screamed. "Damn it!"

The cold air felt like it burrowed into him and sent slithering chills through his body. The pain suddenly tripled as a wave of damp air settled into his bones. Every joint ached with a pulsing, relentless pain. The soreness of attempting even the simplest gestures made him furious.

Rus forced a lurch forward. He yowled as the torturous wrenching of his muscles fought against him. With each step his body convulsed. Rus felt as if a small army raged against him in his own cells.

Rus opened and closed his fists, trying to ease them into moving more fluidly, but they felt stuck. No matter what he tried, his useless body jerked and resisted. Like it had a mind of its own. It felt like trying to control a puppet with wires from ten feet away.

"Crap, this isn't fair. I didn't ask for this," he muttered. Each word came hard as he tried to move, talking and moving at once, seemed too complicated.

Rus finally made it to his feet. "So hungry," he groaned. He looked around as his eyes finally adjusted. *Mary didn't have an old wine cellar, did she?*

Rus felt sure he'd been left for dead in something like a basement. Or a cave. The rough stone walls and dirt floor confirmed the assessment. He noticed a mildewy residue on his hands, probably from something he'd touched. "Wonder how long I've been here."

Rus tapped the wall. "Where the—?" he paused. "Is this the family mausoleum?" He gaped, his eyes searching in the dark for some clue. "No!" his voice echoed. "Maybe I'm asleep? Hallucinating?" He hoped for anything other than what was dawning on him to be true.

"No! No way. It can't be. No one would've put me in here unless I was— I was—" he broke off. Another wave of nausea rippled through him.

"Oh dear God, I'm gonna be sick," he murmured, clutching his side. Rus folded against the wall and retched, his body sweating and shaking as a thick, black liquid oozed from his mouth and pooled at his feet. The stinking rot looked more like it came from the depths of hell than from his gut.

"Oh God, no," Rus howled as another burst of nausea swept over him. He gagged as he heaved up wet chunks of bloody gristle, as if whatever rot had been working through his system finally erupted from him. Freed him.

He closed his eyes and vomited a third time. After a few moments, the feeling of disgust abated. He wiped his mouth gently with his linen sleeve and felt strangely quite relieved.

"Not normal, but better," Rus said. He wiped the muck off his clothes and scraped his hands clean on the moist, stone wall. As he rubbed them, the skin flaked a little more than he'd expected. "What the—?" He hesitated, staring at the black ooze that leaked from him instead of blood, oddly like the liquid that had come from his gut. He patted his still dirty hands on his thin pants and determined to get himself into the light, to see what was the matter.

Rus cocked his head suddenly at a distant sound of movement. Voices nearby. He felt trapped, like an animal, and desperate for any help. "I'm here," he called. "Anyone out there? Can anyone hear me?" he screamed.

"I need to figure a way out of here," Rus stumbled toward a dim crevice light.

***

At Mary's modest split level house, the whole family remained in mourning. Cousins, nephews, neighbours, and friends filled the rooms. From the number of cars in the drive it seemed the home welcomed everyone in a fifty mile radius, gathered to honour the dearly departed. Rus was a capable enough man, well loved, and the sort of fellow whose death hit the whole town hard.

When a knock came on the door, it wasn't a surprise, but the face greeting them was. Mary swung open the door to find the specialist she begged Rus to see, Dr Christi. The good doctor had been out of town at a global health conference. "Dr Christi!" She clasped a hand over her mouth. *He's a very big deal in the healing industry, and here he is at my door. Making a personal appearance, at that.*

Rus's other sister, Martha, moved to the door, staring at the venerable guest. Martha said, "hmph," and frowned at the arrival. Uncle Rory huddled behind them, poking his head between them to see.

Dr Christi stood still as a corpse, his lean body in a tasteful black suit and skinny black tie.

Mary frowned, staring at Christi's face, the suit fit for a funeral. *It was as if he'd known. He'd known. He must've known he was too late.*

Dr Christi's face was rough shaven, but with just enough brown stubble on the chin to appear that he'd come straight from the airport. A mass of thick, dark hair was pulled back in a messy, low pony tail. His features were handsome and kind, almost soft, and the whole effect landed as a sort of intense androgyny. He looked like a dolled up hippy doctor from West Hollywood if he looked like a doctor at all.

"That's the magician doctor?" Uncle Rory hollered from behind the sisters. "Huh! Now I've seen everything!"

Someone yelled, "Shh!" Then a hush fell over the mourning crowd, as all eyes landed on the sisters, waiting to see how they'd reply.

"Well look who it is," Mary whispered. She moved behind Martha, then planted both hands gently on her sister's shoulders. Her surprise turned like bad milk. She added, "Dr Important. Finally showing up after all this!" Mary scowled and deep lines crept across her face. She bit down on her lower lip, chewing, then clucked her tongue at the silent guest.

Martha stood at the door, trembling. She shook her head and sobbed at the sight of him. "Too late," she howled. She ran from the open door, her grey dress flailing behind her. She sunk herself into the sofa amidst a small crowd of friends and sobbed.

Her long-time friend Gary nestled beside her, nudging her into his shoulders. "There, there. Come on now. It was nice of the doctor to come at all. The good doctor must feel terrible about this," Gary said.

"Christi could've saved him," Martha sobbed.

Mary, the older sister, still stood motionless in the doorframe with one arm blocking the entry. Internally she debated whether or not to let him inside. "What good are you now?" she finally snapped.

"I'm sorry I couldn't get here sooner," Dr Christi said. "It's over then?" he asked.

"Quite," Mary said.

"My apologies to Rus, then. To all of you," Dr Christi glanced at the sisters, then turned his face to the other mourners. "For how many days?" Christi asked.

"Four," Mary frowned. "Lord," she said, "I'm sorry, but I think if he'd seen you, my brother wouldn't have died." A smug, self-satisfied smile crossed her face. "How does that make you feel?" she added.

Dr Christi looked at the palm plant sitting on the entry table, and his face went slack. He let out a quiet sigh, and leaning in he touched the thick waxy leaf. His eyes softened, and he said, "Everything rises again. Nothing's ever lost. Not even Rus."

Mary's frown persisted, "Honestly, Doctor, that's not what you expect to hear from a man of science."

"Science, religion. Everything is belief. Do you believe?" he asked.

"In what?" Mary asked. She still stared down at her hands and busied herself folding and unfolding a damp handkerchief, occasionally dabbing at her eyes.

"In life, even after death?" Dr Christi paused, then added, "I think whoever believes will never die." His features were suddenly serious, almost mournful. "Do you believe this?"

Mary's eyes blurred. *Not much by way of explanation, then was it?* After a moment, she released the knot of her brow. She said, "Yes. Lord, yes. Sure. Why not?"

Mary glanced behind her at the room full of mourners. "I want to, anyway," she added. "Look, I believe a lot of things. It's hard to believe he's in a tomb right now. I'd prefer to think of him as free." Mary waved her arms as if she were flying. Suddenly she felt like a foolish child and she settled her wing arms at her side, brushing the dress flat.

Martha rose and walked to the door. They both stared at the doctor, curious about this odd turn to the spiritual.

Martha shrugged, supposing it made a certain kind of sense, since it was too late for cures. She blinked away a tear, then dabbed her dark eyes again.

Dr Christi placed one warm hand on each sister's hand. His pure kindness pulsed through them, delivering a warmth and tenderness they'd never felt. "Let's go to his burial place together," he said. "Now." His voice delivered a blow as firm and final as a coffin nail.

As Mary listened to his smooth voice, she knew she'd follow Dr Christi anywhere. Maybe he was too late, but it was a special compassion he was providing, going to the tomb to mourn together. From the way Martha looked at him, she knew she felt the same way.

"Come in," Mary replied.

Dr Christi entered their home, carrying only a small medical bag.

"Too late for that," Uncle Rory pointed at the bag.

Dr Christi took a deep breath and opened it up. He pulled

out various lotions and instruments and lined them on the table beside the plant. He handed one to Mary. "You'll probably need this." The bottle was filled with a greenish liquid. The hand-written label said,

'SKIN AND BODY WASH'

Mary took it. She squinted at Dr Christi with confusion. She held it up to the light and an odd green light shimmered through the glass.

Uncle Rory frowned, seeing the bottle. "Snake oil salesman," he muttered.

"What?" the doctor asked.

"Well, it's just that," Mary hesitated, "I'm pretty sure if the skin's not on the body, I'm not going to want to wash it."

Martha let out a tight, high laugh. *A relief after all the tears.*

"I'd like to see him," Dr Christi said.

"It's a bit of a drive, but of course," Martha said.

"You may join us," Mary said to the houseful of visitors.

No one who'd made eye contact with the doctor stranger wondered why Mary had made such a strange invitation. Dr Christi had a way about him. Persuasive to the point of magnetic.

The guests who'd seen Christi's face gathered at their cars, curious.

But the other guests sped home, relieved to get back to their lives, football games, calls to make. Life went on. Rus was a good guy, but there was only so much friends could do. Christi himself said, "Everything rises." It was time for them to do just that.

Dr Christi escorted the sisters to his car, opening the doors for them first, then slid across from them.

"Where have you set him to rest?" he asked.

"A family tomb at the Holy Acres Cemetery," Mary said.

Dr Christi nodded. "Of course," his voice smooth as silk.

Martha shot Mary an angry glance. She pinched her eyes closed, tired of competing for attention, and laid her head back on the headrest.

Dr Christi's driver put on some classical music. Martha crossed her hands in her laps, opened her eyes, and vowed to be silent for the ride. Dr Christi tapped on the glass, and the driver started the car. He stared straight at them, and said, "I'm so deeply sorry."

They both felt and knew that he was. Their hearts softened a second time when he took each of their hands. Seated across from them, Dr Christi bowed his head and prayed.

They started to pray with him. Then Dr Christi wept.

Mary stared at him, blushing. *What a guy.* She said, "Everyone loved Rus! Have you ever seen so many mourners?"

Martha's sister snapped, "Could you have kept Rus from dying?" Immediately, a flash of shame turned her face pink, and she corrected herself, "I'm sorry." Then she cried so hard she couldn't stop.

Dr Christi felt troubled and moved by their grief. He sighed. His breath sounded strained, like his own heart might burst from their pain. When they arrived at the cemetery, they drove through the iron gates in silence. A few cars followed behind, those friends who'd decided they were curious about this funny doctor.

Mary pointed to the family section, and the driver parked

near the tomb. They exited the car, each lost in thought, and stepped across the hallowed ground. The friends emptied from their cars and followed. When they reached the family plot, Dr Christi stepped to the tomb, setting a hand on the entrance. "Open up the door. Move away the stones," he said.

"Hell no! He's rotting in there. Leave him!" Mary pleaded, suddenly confused about the plan.

Dr Christi, still calm, said, "Did I not tell you that if you believe, you will rise again?"

"This is crazy talk. Comforting us is one thing. But, come on. I thought you just wanted to visit the tomb! To pray! You can't be serious!" Martha stood clutching her sister's arm, united in resistance.

Dr Christi turned to the few who'd joined them. "Do it," he said. Once he set his eyes on their friends, they complied. Together they stood at the stone door.

Dr Christi looked up and recited a quiet prayer.

Uncle Rory looked around. Everyone strained and leaned into the door, but it didn't budge. Rory tried to listen to the prayer, but couldn't quite recognise it. Sounded like an awful lot of pleading divination, like his whole medical reputation landed on this one act of weirdness. *Whoever this guy is, he definitely has a funny kind of God complex, like a lot of big doctors get, I guess.*

The door opened.

Rory picked out the last part "by a divine hand... that they may believe... " then Dr Christi's voice trailed off again. *Charlatan*, Rory thought.

Dr. Christi commanded in a loud voice, "Rus! Come out!" His voice echoed in the hollow tomb.

***

The dead man came from the tomb, feet still draped with strips of linen, and a dirty cloth swinging from the waist, draped over wobbling legs.

Rus rubbed his eyes as if the sunlight scorched. He looked around, eager to be freed from the nightmare. *Was I buried alive?*

Sisters and friends surrounded Rus. For a second, he felt pure relief, but then he noticed that mostly, they were screaming.

Rus looked down at his body and saw the mess of himself. Greyish limbs flailing, the cuts on his hand still oozing black slime, his face torn and patched with scabby crust. He knew the streaks of vomit must still be smeared across his lips. *Jesus. It's not like I had a mirror and dressing room in there. What the hell's wrong with you people?*

His sisters looked red eyed and pale, and rather like they were about to vomit. Rus realized he probably smelled from the faces they were making. *But shouldn't they be... happier?*

Rus stared at the Doctor, familiar from the infomercials, the ones that made Mary push him to get recruited as a test subject. He tried to smile, but his chapped lips hurt too much. *What's he doing here?*

"Aaoh," Rus screamed, staggering from the darkness. He was elated to see his family, a few friends. His steps were still jagged, and he struggled to coordinate motion and speech. *But they'd rescued him! Thank God, he'd been saved!*

Rus stared at them, expecting their warmth. Relief. But he suspected something a lot worse was going on from the way they stared.

Martha gasped at the sight of him, then covered her mouth and nose with her hand, gagging. She looked repulsed.

Mary shrieked and took a big step back. She went greenish. She suddenly wished she hadn't eaten all that casserole at the wake.

Then the screaming.

Rus's dear friends shuddered and shrank back to their cars, embarrassed by their curiosity. They ran, averting their eyes.

"Oh God!"

"Why'd we follow that weirdo?"

"Damn hippy doctor!"

A few onlookers swarmed toward them.

Rus felt angry. Then terrified as the ones he loved recoiled and strangers dotted the landscape to see about the fuss, to see what was the matter. He was the matter. He suddenly began to doubt that he'd been buried alive. More like he'd risen from the dead. But that was impossible. *Come on, man. Really?*

"Whe-e-e-re you-u-u go-o?" Rus howled after his dearly departed friends. He lunged toward them, dragging each leg forward. He tried to stop them. "Wa-a-ait," his mouth felt clogged. It was hard to talk and move, the pain was so bad. He reached out his arms, desperate.

Every step felt like being pounded with a hammers from every direction. His legs ached as they wobbled. He flung out arms trying to balance with every step. *Should I at least say thanks?* However they'd found him, it was a flipping miracle alright. Or a nightmare.

"No-o go-o!" he yelled, confused as they scattered away. *Leaving without at least a hello?* He couldn't help the condition he was in. *Wasn't my doing.* He took another look at himself. He was a wreck and quite sure he'd not been buried alive.

91

Rus stared at the doctor and stood still. At least he mastered standing. He could do this. *It's just going to take time. And medicine. Maybe that's why the doctor had come. Maybe there's a cure.* A smile broadened on his face.

Only Uncle Rory and the sisters remained at Dr Christi's side. Rory was too petrified by the sight of his sluggish, half-naked, and mostly dead nephew flailing in the sunlight to move. The stench alone should've made him run, but he planted his hands on his hips and stared, mouth wide open as a flycatcher.

Dr Christi was the only calm. He opened the medical bag and tossed a pair of sweatpants to Rus. Dr Christi yelled, "Take off your grave clothes."

Rus clamoured for them, arms flapping as he lurched in those uneven steps.

"What's wrong with him?" Mary asked, trembling.

Rus clutched the sweatpants and splattered to the ground, his legs spread, landing in a heap. He shoved one leg in at a time, grateful for the chance to cover himself. Maybe some of the bruises and marks were too much for his sisters. After he'd dressed, he pushed onto all fours, then carefully pressed up onto his wobbling legs.

"Thanks," Rus said. His voice seemed clearer. Then he took a faltering step and yowled, wincing in pain.

"He's hurt," Martha exclaimed.

Dr Christi's face beamed at the sight of the stumbling Rus. For a moment, his smile seemed full of a pride and confidence. His bright eyes twinkled. Everything in his face pronounced, *Yes, I'm the miracle worker you know me to be.* Then his expression darkened. His brow knotted, and he looked to the sisters. He pointed at the cemetery, all those graves and tombs. His eyes flashed, and without a word, he seemed to offer some kind of message. A warning.

"Do you want to examine him?" Mary asked.

"No. He's fine. Let him go." Dr Christi smiled. A small crowd of onlookers gathered near the tomb. For a moment, he wondered about the best way to deliver the news.

"Well, what now?" Martha asked.

Dr Christi asked, "Look, are there about twelve hours of daylight?"

"Um, sure. Yes," Mary said.

"Is this going to be a parable?" Rory huffed.

"Look," Dr Christi pointed at Rus, now only a few feet away.

They all looked.

Dr Christi puffed up his chest and nodded toward Rus, "Anyone who walks in the daytime will not stumble, for they see by the sunlight. It is when a person walks at night that they stumble, for they have no light."

"What?" Rory asked. Dr Christi sounded like he was on a bit of a soapbox. "You saying his eyes just need to adjust?"

Dr Christi stayed quiet.

"Well that hardly explains the reek," Rory added, frowning.

Rus noticed as people neared, the urge to eat grew. He licked his lips as he stared, then let out a wild, primal groan.

"He must've been alive in there. Buried alive. What a nightmare," Mary said.

"He can see now," Dr Christi said.

"Oh God," Mary said.

Rus stumbled toward Martha, reaching for her.

Martha recoiled, mouth twisted in revulsion.

Rus stood perfectly still, hoping he could make contact.

"Well, on the bright side, he's not dead now," Rory said. The strangers who'd come to see the disturbance at the cemetery either froze or ran at the explanation. Dozens scrambled to get away.

"It's *him*!" Martha pointed at Dr Christi. "*He* did this!" she shouted.

"Freak!" Mary screamed at the doctor.

I'd watch who's calling who a freak, Rus thought.

Rus moved toward the doctor, who seemed like the only one not panicked. He hoped for an answer. A cure. Anything to quell the pain. The hunger.

Dr Christi's eyes sparkled in the sunlight. "You see, he is yet alive," he said. Then he stepped close to the undead Rus and pointed toward the people nearest the tomb. The onlookers were transfixed by the sight of such a spectacle. "Listen," Dr Christi whispered to Rus, "I've got to go, but trust me. I don't want to say what, but you really need something to eat."

Zombies on Film

Straight to DVD

By Dan Pawley

VOICE OF ANTHONY HARDING ('The Reverend Davis'):

Ah, hello. I expect you've come to interview me? Lovely, lovely. I don't suppose you get many famous actors around here, do you? This whole thing must be terrifically exciting for you, just like the circus coming to town. Lucky for you, you weren't here earlier on. We had this terrible fog on set, just came out of nowhere. Gone now, of course. Got a few of the extras coughing, but no harm done really. I suppose that's what we get for filming out in the sticks, eh? No offence meant of course, it's just that I'm used to theatre land. Very different environment. Oh, I do wander on, don't I? I suppose I should talk about this film. Just between you and me, it's the most dreadful rubbish. I'm only doing it as a favour to my agent really. Lovely lady, works so hard, likes a drink a little more than she should if you know what I mean. Anyway, where was I? Oh yes, this one. Tosh, darling, tosh with a capital T. And I should know. Why, I've been doing horror practically before I could walk. I did Hammer, Amicus, all the greats. Vincent and I, we had some times. Oh, and Christopher – what a joker! These days, all they want is gore. Lashings of blood and some tits, and they're happy. No suspense, no proper scares, not anymore. I mean, look at that extra over there. Covered in blood, and is that supposed to be some sort of internal organ hanging out of his mouth? Not exactly subtle, is it? Oh look, here he comes. I suppose he's going to pester me for an autograph. Still, always be nice to the help, that's what I say. Let me rummage around for a pen... oh I say... what are you doing? Wha—

HOLLY SEYMOUR, junior reporter:

And that's where the tape stops. Thank God I had the presence of mind to remember my Dictaphone. I don't know how, I must have been just functioning automatically even though I was in shock. Before all this, I didn't really know who Harding was, I was just looking for a bit of background after my editor had told me to get a couple of pages if I could, because he'd already maxed out on the Lower Thrumpington vegetable competition and still had half the paper to fill. I checked him out on IMDB, and well, I don't like to speak ill of the dead, but the closest he'd ever got to Hammer or Vincent Price was third pitchfork on the left in some terrible sixties movie. Spent most of his career in provincial repertory, trousers forever falling down when the vicar came to tea, that kind of thing.

Anyway, I don't think I'll ever forget that jet of blood as the extra bit into Anthony's neck. I'm just glad I was sat on the other side of him. I was wearing my best blouse and bloodstains can be so difficult to get out, can't they? So I grabbed the phone and just ran. There were more of them coming out of the canteen, blood and all sorts down their fronts. It was chaos. People were running and screaming, and these things just kept coming. They were grabbing whomever they could and biting into them. One runner tried to fight back with a clapperboard. He sliced off its nose, but the monster didn't even wince. It just seized him and bit right into his shoulder. I don't think he made it. There was so much blood everywhere, you couldn't tell who was eating and who was being eaten. The creatures were slow, though, and that saved my life, being able to run away. I did slip on puddles of blood a few times, but I managed to get back to my car, and hightail it out of there.

I know there are some who would think it was a bit off for me to run away while an eighty year old man was being eaten, but I was thinking of the wider public. They deserve to know. I was just serving the cause of journalism really. I'm a very lucky girl. I mean, in many ways it was absolutely horrible, but it was also kind of a gift, right? This could be my big break, the story that gets me into the big leagues. I've already been on the BBC, and now you guys. You don't know anyone in your HR department, do you? Anyone to do with recruitment?

MITCH JENKINS, producer:

I'm not going to lie to you. It was a rubbish movie. I knew it was rubbish. The director knew it was rubbish. Even the writer knew it was rubbish, and writers don't know anything, present company excepted, haha.

My outfit turns out fifty of these a year. Horror, war, gangsters, you name it, we'll do it quick, and we'll do it cheap. Do a quick edit, pull some box art off the shelf, get it into Tesco, and we'll do ten thousand units a month, and soak up all the tax breaks while we're at it. Don't know why I ever thought of doing anything else, this is easy money right here.

Anyway, I'm not a very hands-on producer. Let the director do what he wants, as long as he comes in on time and under budget. That's my style. I don't even go on set that much, but I decided to visit that day. I had a dirty weekend in the country booked with the girlfriend – don't tell the wife, haha – and I figured if I could get there a bit earlier and pay a visit, I could call it work and claim the petrol on expenses.

So there I was on set, little canvas chair and all, and it's going swimmingly. I'm talking to Roger, the director, may he rest in peace, and everything's peachy. We're on the same wavelength. I've got a good feeling about the whole thing. I think I'll hang around, watch the next scene, and then make myself scarce before lunchtime. Roger says it's a good one, the first monster attack. So I sit back to watch, and I tell you, when that first creature appeared, I nearly hit the flipping roof. It just looked too good. Normally our monsters are all rubber and tomato sauce, but this one was way above that. Jesus, Roger, I remember shouting at him, how much have you spent on this? Are you trying to bankrupt me? No, wait, this isn't right, says Roger, I'll go and investigate. So off he marches, over to this beast that's costing me an arm and a leg, and the bleeding thing only goes and takes a chomp out of his cheek, doesn't it? Couldn't believe it. I'm standing there gawping while this thing's chewing on bits of my director. I was out of there like a rocket. Nearly spoilt my whole weekend, it did. No way I could get it up that night. But Natalie turned up trumps with some of those little blue pills, so it wasn't a total write-off in the end.

DAVID SMITHERS, rambler:

We'd been walking on the Downs earlier, up near the Army base. It's not on the maps, but everyone round here knows that's what it is. We were skirting round that tall fence when we saw this cloud coming out of one of the chimneys in there. It was a thick, yellowy colour, like mustard gas. Not that I've ever seen mustard gas, but that's what I imagine it would be like. Of course, at the time we didn't think it was anything bad. I remember saying to Brenda that I was sure it was safe. They wouldn't be allowed to pump it out if it wasn't, would they? She said it was going to blow in the direction of the film set we'd passed earlier, and she hoped it didn't ruin their filming for the day. Our boy's home from university now, and he was hoping to get some work there as an extra. We just thank our lucky stars he didn't, don't we Brenda?

Now they're saying it was some chemical spill, some kind of nasty superweapon they were testing that got loose down there. When I think of all those poor people, well, I'm a mild-mannered man, but it makes my blood boil. And then the planes and missiles they used to end it all? It was like ten Guy Fawkes Nights rolled into one. The dog still hasn't come out from under the spare bed. We're not happy, not happy at all. This is going to cost a fortune in pet therapy, and who's paying? That's what I want to know.

MAJOR IAN MORRISS, MOD spokesman:

The Ministry is of course fully aware of the recent tragic events on the set of [checks notes] *Teen Zombie Beach Party 2: The Awakening*. I can assure you that an internal investigation will be conducted, but I should also inform you that in the interests of national security, it is highly unlikely the results will ever be published. In the meantime, we should all salute the quick and courageous actions of our pilots, who ensured that this incident was bought to a conclusion without any further loss of life. I will not be taking any further questions. Thank you and goodnight.

MITCH JENKINS, producer:

You might think I'd be angry about all this. Nah. Any problem is just an opportunity in disguise, that's what my old man always said. It's a shame about Roger and the others, but let's face it – I can get a director and crew straight out of film school and pay them half what Roger was on. Every cloud and all that. Plus there's a whopping payment coming from the insurance company. And best of all, the cameraman had the presence of mind to keep rolling. That reminds me, I must find out his name, send some flowers to the widow. It's the right thing to do, isn't it? Thanks to him I've got the best monster effects I've ever had, and the explosion to end all explosions for the final reel. Okay, the UK market's probably out for the time being, but I've got international buyers queuing up. Mark my words, this is the start of something big!

Green Zombie

By Jon Charles

Well, yeah, after paying out for four years of film school my folks had hopes of my working on something with Meryl Streep in, but I always liked horror movies. And it was four weeks filming in the Caribbean. Okay, I was just going to be the Clapper Girl – please, don't, I've heard all those jokes – but you've got to start somewhere in the movie business.

And, anyway, doing the clapper board is great experience. I'm there for every shot. I see how the director works. I see what the actors do differently each take. I see everything. It's the best finishing class you can get. And I got paid too. Not much, really, seeing as how this was a pretty low-budget movie. I think the cost of flying us down to the Dominican Republic blew half the budget but the director swore that he had found a way of making the movie look like it cost more than it actually would. Maybe that's when I should have started to wonder.

I went in eyes open. I know how this kind of thing works. The script was called 'Green Zombie.' Zach, the writer was a fan of that old Bela Lugosi film 'White Zombie' and had written an updated movie. You know, what they call a re-imagining; which is really just a pretentious way of saying remake. There was some kind of problem with the title so Don came up with the idea of adding some aliens and changing white to green. In this version the Lugosi part is an alien in disguise trying to trigger a zombie apocalypse in order to wipe humans from the planet to make way for an alien colonisation. Yeah, I know, kinda cheesy. And that's before you get to the nude scenes. I mean this film was set in the Caribbean but all four female speaking roles were white actresses and they all had to sign a contract agreeing to show their boobs. It's like the 70s never went away.

The first week went okay. It was mostly the daylight scenes at the hotel and beach; all the stuff where everyone still looks clean and healthy. No effects shots yet and nothing with the zombies yet. We were right on schedule. Don never seemed to need more than four takes on anything. Most nights we were finished, showered and in the hotel bar by 9pm; which is early for a location shoot.

It was on the eighth day that things started to go weird. We drove up into the hills where Don said he'd found a really cool location. We drove for three hours, along tracks that got narrower and steeper and more overgrown by the mile. Finally we pulled up at a pair of shacks in a clearing. An old local guy waved to us from a hammock strung between two poles on the porch of one of the shacks. He was drinking from a Mountain Dew bottle but I think it probably held a still drink, if you know what I mean. Don and the AD went over to talk to him while the rest of us just stumbled out and stretched.

According to the shooting schedule we were due to film a couple of scenes here, including one in which the zombies first appear. That turned out to be the second scene of the day. It was starting to get dark and Don called for the camera, sound and lighting guys, and me, to follow him down an old trail path. Ten minutes in we reached a small clearing where there were a bunch of guys just sort of standing. As we got closer I could hear them moaning. They didn't really look like most of the zombies that you've seen in films. They looked a bit more alive; more tragic, as if they were in pain at the loss of their humanity. I thought it seemed a neat idea on Don's part to get away from the cliché. At least that was my first guess.

Don whispered to us that these were real, actual zombies. People who had been registered dead but still walked around. He'd seen it on some kind of 'strange but true' TV show and decided that it would be a cheap way of filming zombie scenes. No make up needed and no payment to the zombies themselves.

We did a hand held camera job filming the zombies from

every angle we could think of. Don tried a close up which worked a treat. This one zom just stared into the camera with a real melancholy kinda look on his face, then he lurched forward to try and eat the lens. After we were done Don got a bunch of pigs livers out of a cool box and threw them out for the zombies. In retrospect that might have been a mistake.

So far so good but I was curious about how we were going to do the scenes with the real (by which I mean paid) actors. I was starting to guess the obvious but I hoped I was wrong.

The next two days we did some scenes in another part of the jungle which mostly involved Rob and Julie, the two leads, running around and shooting guns. For some reason Julie had to wear high heels and a bikini.

We had a day off after that while Don drove up into the hills again, only this time with just the location manager and in a transit van they'd hired locally. The rest of us hung out by the pool and I finally managed to get some time with Zach. We talked about movie scripts to begin with and he was encouraging me to write stuff. Later we walked along the beach and, can you believe it, we actually watched the sunset together. I mean I know that happens in movies all the time but never in real life. He told me all about the projects he was working on and what he really wanted to do. He was a smart guy. Too good for 'Green Zombie.'

I shared a room at the hotel with the make up girl so Zach asked if I wanted to go up to his room. We were on his balcony kissing when I felt a hand reach up my top. I would've been cool with that if it weren't that I could already feel two hands on my ass. I pulled away from Zach and saw one of the zombies faces right behind him only now Zach looked the less alive as there was an arm punched right through his chest from back to front. Seeing it could no longer reach me it settled for Zach's heart which it pulled right out and started eating. Zach's script said zombies ate brains. Turns out they like to vary their menus.

103

I ran out of the room and slammed the door shut behind me. Julie came running out from Don's room and I guessed, from her screams, that Don wouldn't be following any time soon. There were screams coming from somewhere else in the hotel as well.

You probably saw the rest on CNN. People died. The local police arrived. The zooms got rounded up and herded off to some prison somewhere.

What you don't know is that during the chaos I grabbed hold of all the film. There's enough here that it could be put together as a found footage movie. Just needs a bit of editing.

So, what do you say? Will you give me the money?

The Real Monsters

Apocalypse How

By Shannon Hollinger

Spencer Chapman always knew he'd make all the sadistic teenagers who terrorized him in high school pay. At the time he didn't know how, or when, only that he'd get the job done. And he did. He didn't like to boast, but being the creator of the zombie apocalypse wasn't anything to thumb your nose at. Sure, he didn't do it the way everyone expected it to happen, the way movies and TV and books told of, with droves of dead people roaming the streets looking for brains, but a zombie apocalypse was a zombie apocalypse, wasn't it?

The idea had first taken root while he was trapped within the confines of a locker in high school. Not his meticulously neat and tidy locker, but a jock's locker, thick with the stench of sour sweat and expired lunch meat. Spencer had peered through the vents, watching the other kids mill about, oblivious to his predicament. They went about their business, each with their own important little task. That's when he first drew the comparison between people and cockroaches. After Spencer had managed to catch the attention of a passing custodian to come to his assistance, the idea slipped from his mind, but he would later distinctly remember that time as the day his plan began to form.

It wasn't until years later, while watching a horde of red-eyed lab mice scurrying about their tank, that the memory returned. He'd inherited his parent's house after their untimely passing. A freak lawnmower accident for his father, followed by Spencer giving his mother a little extra assistance down the stairs, and then it was all his. The glorious basement where he had spent the better part of his youth was finally the private sanctuary where he could conduct his experiments without interruption.

For years he had tried to work from whatever crappy little apartment he was living in at the time, but there were just too many distractions. He had always known that the basement was where he would give birth to his greatest achievement. Just like Spencer had always known that he would eventually have to rid the world of the misery that was his parents. With everything lining up just as he knew it would, he moved forward with his plan.

Infectious diseases had always been his passion. Sure, he spent most of his time trying to cure them while working for the CDC, but that was just how he paid the bills until the time came to devote his efforts to the art of creation. After his parent's demise, he quit his job to focus on his real purpose in life – to make his mark on the world, altering the course of humankind forever.

Spencer had considered using a disease like Ebola, something that would have the dramatically pleasing effects of cells turning to mush as their hosts bled from every pore. A bad late night horror movie, however, changed his course. He became fixated on America's obsession with a pending zombie apocalypse. They seemed so excited about it; to eagerly anticipate its arrival. Why not give the people what they wanted?

That's when he turned his attention from petri dishes to mice. Although the mice had a physiology similar enough to humans to achieve his purpose, he found something dissatisfying about using them as his hosts. Mice just seemed so trite. He thought about using rats, which were a better analogy for his feelings about humans, but they had been the carriers of the Black Plague, so he felt it had been done already. He needed a host that made more of a statement. That's when the long-forgotten idea was remembered. What better social commentary for his views on humanity than to use cockroaches? They were perfect, not just from a symbolic perspective, but from an evolutionary standpoint as well. Roaches could survive a savage stomping, live submerged in water for half an hour, eat their way through walls – hell, some of them could even fly. A nuclear blast couldn't even end their reign.

It took a bit of finagling to get his viral strain to take hold in the insects while also remaining transmutable to humans, but in the end, Spencer succeeded. He knew he had created the perfect monster. Human zombies had been portrayed as both fast and slow, but never smart. They couldn't strategize, they couldn't plot, they didn't intentionally hide – they were just there. But roaches... roaches were one of evolution's most prized creatures. Roaches hadn't just survived for millions of years. They had thrived.

Spencer released his vengeance and watched as the vast majority of the population fell quickly. Most people hadn't even realized that roaches could bite, and while the incubation period for the transmission of the disease from host to human took only 48 hours, many humans never made it into zombie-hood. Those who did reach zombie status were preyed upon and consumed by zombie roaches.

The challenge for survival wasn't avoiding rabid dead people with a cannibalistic taste for brain or trying to sneak into towns undetected for supplies. It was going to the bathroom. It was eating. It was bathing or changing clothes or doing anything that involved exposing skin. Spencer had, of course, inoculated himself against the virus. The blood that coursed through his veins carried an additive that made him unappetizing to bite. He had no trouble at all moving about however he wished, unmolested.

But Spencer had succeeded too well. Once he was the last of his kind, he missed watching people, instead of roaches, rushing about on their way, scurrying about on their important errands. He was surrounded by nothing but insects, savage as they destroyed everything that was left of humanity around him in their insatiable appetite for destruction. Spencer realized the true commentary, and the irony was not lost upon him. He was alone in a world of cockroaches, and he was their king.

Family Ties

By Stephen Blake

The smell from the chimney had been getting worse since Christmas Eve. We'd all gotten up early Christmas morning and rushed down to see the presents under the tree.

As the eldest it was my job to squeeze in between the fireplace and the tree and turn on the lights. It was as I lay there reaching toward the switch, that the smell really hit me. I'd only been allowed home from the clinic for Christmas and even though the odour was rancid, I preferred it to the disinfected smell I normally dealt with.

Dad turned up bleary eyed ten minutes after us. "It's just some bird that's died in the chimney," he assured us. My two sisters, twins and only four years old, burst into tears at the thought of a bird dead in our chimney. Dad was his usual tactful self, "Well, alright, maybe it's a squirrel then." Cue howls of tears from Molly and Abigail.

Mum arrived from the kitchen and sprayed so much air freshener about the place we thought we might choke on the stuff.

We abandoned the sitting room during Boxing Day. On the 27th Dad decided to try and do something about it. He went to see a neighbour whom he knew owned some chimney sweep brushes. He came back looking very concerned.

"Mr Jones reckons there has been some sort of worldwide disaster," he said shaking his head. "He reckons the dead are rising from the grave and eating people."

Mum chided him, "Don't be daft. He's pulling your leg."

"I need to look online," he stated.

Dad had promised Mum faithfully not to go online over Christmas, and since we had only had the telly on to watch

DVDs, we'd not actually seen any news in days.

Molly and Abigail played blissfully. Me, I looked over Dad's shoulder and saw some of the footage that showed the attacks by the undead. "Cool," I muttered. Dad looked at me disapprovingly. I don't know what he expected. The psychiatrists have told him over and over I am 'removed' from the world. I look at him wearily. I want to scream, 'So I'm weird, odd, and maybe dead inside – deal with it,' but I merely smile, knowing that always leaves him feeling disconcerted.

A quick scan of the government advice confirmed that virtually everything we'd ever seen in a horror movie was true. I nodded as I read it. "I knew it," I cried, "I told Danny West zombies can't run. They do shuffle slowly."

My parents had a look of disbelief as I punched the air, my intellectual victory confirmed.

Dad turned to mum, "Christ, my father. He was meant to come and see the kids. He was going to dress up in a Santa suit."

"Father Christmas," I corrected him.

Mum tutted, "Stop it with these little comments and help me get what we can from the garage to barricade the house."

I rolled my eyes, but chastened, I did as I was told and went with her to gather every little bit of wood we could muster.

A few hours later the house seemed impenetrable. Only I doubt it really was, it just seemed it.

Dad couldn't get hold of Granddad. Dad asked who saw him last. My parents' eyes fell upon me accusingly. I sighed, "We chatted about making his entrance authentic. I helped him."

After a lot of tears and hugs – my parents, not me – Dad

went out to drive the two miles to get to Granddad's flat.

Mum decided to be pro-active and do something about the smell in the sitting room, just in case we all needed to stay there for safety.

She put down some old bed sheets and untied the brushes. I helped screw together the length of it, and Mum began to push it up the chimney.

It didn't get very far before it reached the blockage. She pushed and pulled, but whatever it was did not want to budge.

I handed her a torch, and she leaned into the fireplace. We'd not used it for years, but it hadn't been blocked up.

Mum clicked the torch on. I only know that she let out a brief scream. It was there, piercing, and then abruptly not there. Her legs stuck out the fireplace, twitching.

I grabbed her ankles and pulled. She moved a little and then seemed to jerk back into the chimney. With all my strength I heaved and managed to pull her out of the fireplace. Holding onto her was my Granddad, dressed as old Saint Nick himself. Still alive, Mum's hands grasped for something to hold onto. She managed to grab a tree branch but since it was a fake tree it just broke free. She reached again and this time held onto the string of Christmas lights. She held onto them like someone would who had been thrown a rope whilst stuck in quicksand.

She was dead now. I could tell by the fact Granddad was munching on her face. I should have been distraught but, well, I wasn't. I looked at Granddad and asked him, "Would you like a twiglet or maybe an orange and lemon slice?"

He ignored me and continued to feast on Mum. Slightly dazed, I left the room and got the chains we'd got out of the garage earlier. Dad had bought them thinking we could stop all of the family bikes being stolen if they were tied together.

I sniggered at the thought of zombie gangs riding my little sisters' bikes with the stabilisers on. I ran up to my parents' room and looked in Mum's bedside cabinet. I knew this was where she and Dad kept their matching handcuffs.

With Granddad distracted whilst he ate, I shackled his legs and waist. I tied it off to the bolts we still had in the ceiling and floor from when Dad was on a fitness kick and had bought himself a punch bag. It had been put in various places around the house. The bolts and links now proved very useful.

Happy that Granddad was secure I went to the kitchen and made him some gravy. I returned and poured it on what was left of Mum for him.

I'd not heard Dad return and so when he started wailing in the sitting room, it did surprise me.

He screwed his face up and shouted, "What have you done? Don't you understand this isn't right?"

I looked at him and suddenly realising what he meant, I felt ashamed. I ran passed him and quickly returned with a jar of cranberry sauce for Granddad. "I'm so sorry," I said, speaking to both of them. "It was thoughtless of me."

I think Dad might have been upset. He left with my sisters and for some reason didn't want either myself or Granddad to come along.

For quite some time I was really unsure about what to do. It was Granddad who gave me the idea. When he'd finished eating Mum, he was quiet for almost a day, and then he started to make some noises. Initially it was just a moan, then a kind of growl and well, all of a sudden he seemed to embrace the role. I swear, he looked at me and said, "Huh, huh, huh." I remember looking at him quizzically, and then he tried again, and there it was. "Ho, Ho, Ho!" Or something close to it.

I'd found my calling. I started immediately redecorating the outside of the house. I daubed sheets with the words 'Safe Haven' and 'Grotto.' I put up lights, did a little display with reindeers and a sled. I managed to make them out of leftover bones – just so the sitting room doesn't get untidy. It's very creative if I say so myself.

We get young and old coming to the house. I don't judge, I leave that to Granddad. He decides if they are naughty or nice. I just send them in. Unfortunately we've not had any good ones so far, but I've faith in people. I know some well-behaved, nice people will call round. The zombies don't really bother us. They seem to nod and shuffle away.

Granddad is doing alright, hanging together – just about. He looks even more festive nowadays. The string of lights Mum had held onto has passed right through him now, still plugged into the wall. Good job they're LED's. They look really pretty running from the tree, into his mouth and out his arse.

I've got myself a name badge saying Father Christmas's helper. It said Santa but I corrected that. I feel it's important that I stay and help Granddad. After all it was me that killed him and shoved him up the chimney. Who knew he'd come back as a zombie? I really feel a family connection to him. We've more in common now than ever before; monsters together.

Forlorn Hope

By Anthony Watson

We're closer to the centre of town now and there are more of them out there on the sidewalks. We have to get this right, it's not like we can have too many attempts and it's a case of getting the balance right between too many and too few. Too many and we're putting all of us in danger needlessly – I feel secure enough inside the BearCat but there's no need to push our luck, just because we've always been okay before doesn't mean that's always going be the case, there's a first time for everything. Too few and we could end up wasting our time, all that work for nothing.

We're in the 'burbs now though and the numbers seem just about right.

Even after all this time it's still strange to see these empty streets. (Not completely empty of course, but *emptier...*) Before it all happened there'd be kids out playing, people going about their day to day business. There'd be more vehicles on the roads than just the armoured car we're in right now. And, of course, *they* wouldn't be there.

Just that slight tilt of their heads as we pass them, just enough to let us know that *they* know we're here. Still creeps me out to see it, even though I know why they do it, or at least *think* I know.

I hear the revs of the engine decreasing, the BearCat's slowing. I can see where the driver is going to pull up. It's a good choice, out in the open with a good enough distance from the nearest of them.

I turn to look at Daniel but he doesn't see or acknowledge me, just stares out the window.

***

We went into lockdown long before the media got a hold

of what was going on. By the time the first news reports, with jerky, hand-held footage of the rampages in the streets, hit the screens, we'd secured the whole complex and were already planning our strategy.

Our first teleconference with the President was fraught with tension, the HD monitor clearly showing the stress and strain in his face as he spoke to us from the Oval Office.

"What's your assessment of the *situation*?" was naturally one of his first questions, the way he said it putting those inverted commas around 'situation.'

We'd given our 'assessment' based as it was on that same footage the rest of the world was now watching but also on more precise and specific information provided by our field operatives. No explanations of course, not then – how could you possibly explain those acts of violence, those attacks on men, women and children, *by* men, women and children, that rendered flesh and spilt blood in such quantities? How too to *explain* how, minutes after an attack, the victims got to their feet and began their own trail of mayhem.

No explanations then, just theories.

"All signs point to it being a virus," Professor Elsevier told the President, his voice calm and measured despite the intensity of the situation, "one that renders the infected extremely aggressive whilst at the same time making them – somehow – resilient to injury and damage."

The President didn't respond to that one immediately, merely steepled his fingers and rested his chin on them, a gesture we'd all seen so many times before on TV, a gesture that had always conveyed the impression of a deep thinker, a man who *cared*. It struck me at that precise moment that it was a damn fine piece of acting, a distraction to give himself time to think. Given that the thoughts running through his head right then must have been along the lines of *'oh fuck, it's the end of the world, what do I do now?'* I was particularly impressed. An Oscar-winning performance.

Slowly he raised his head from his hands and stared directly into the camera to ask another question.

"Is it one of ours?"

***

I clamber into the back of the BearCat and place a hand on Daniel's shoulder. He still hasn't stopped looking out of the window, still hasn't acknowledged my presence. I give a gentle squeeze and he turns slowly to face me. His eyes seem un-focussed, like he's been in some kind of trance (and who would blame him for finding whatever means of escape he can) but gradually he comes back to himself and a smile plays across his lips.

"Daz!" he says, as if this is some kind of reunion of long lost pals (and I take it as a good sign that he hasn't called me Darius, something he only does when he's stressed or angry). And then I find that I can't speak. I'd come back here to give some final words of reassurance, to give him one last chance to change his mind but suddenly my mouth has become so dry I can't physically form words – not that there are any in my head anyway.

"It's fine," he says, and reaches out to squeeze *my* shoulder. It's a touching gesture but one that fills me with guilt, this isn't how it's supposed to work.

"You can still—"

"I know," he interrupts, "but I won't." He grips my other shoulder with his other hand, grips *really* tightly, "this is what we've worked for, this is too important to back out now."

I nod, unable again to find words. Everything he says is true, I can't argue with that but there's a world of difference between planning something, discussing it in abstract terms and actually doing it. More than I ever knew...

"They're beginning to move." The voice comes from behind

116

me, from the driver, "we need to hurry."

My stomach twists in on itself at the words, hot acid floods my oesophagus and my eyes tear up at the burning pain. Oh shit, this is it. I feel another squeeze on my shoulders and look back at Daniel. He's staring intently at me but the look isn't aggressive, it's one of understanding, of compassion – of a man at peace with himself. I envy him that if nothing else. He nods, once, quickly and gets up off his seat.

*****

It *wasn't* one of ours, that was the one thing we could tell the President with any degree of certainty. We did, of course, discuss whose it might be because at that time bio-terrorism was still the likeliest explanation. At that time we only knew about what was going on here, in the States. As time went on, and it became apparent that this was a world-wide problem, we came to realise that this was a natural event and not the result of mankind's interference and the focus switched entirely to investigating the infection itself.

What was it? Could it be cured? The two questions – the two most important questions in the world – became a mantra. Of course, in order to answer those questions we needed material to research.

Early attempts to capture the infected were less than satisfactory. The rage that was one of the defining characteristics of the contagion proved to be a major obstacle in the apprehension of subjects. After the first few unsuccessful forays, urgent operational meetings were held with our military colleagues to devise a strategy.

"At least we know we can cure them," I remember one of the soldiers saying, "blow their heads off and they stop attacking for sure."

Some laughter greeted this comment, all from the Army's side of the table.

And yet, from such crass beginnings, a plan did emerge. True, headshots put the infected down – in truth it was the *only* way to achieve this – but gunshot wounds to other parts of the body, no matter how severe, did not kill them.

They did slow them down though and, (even now I cannot get over how surreal this sounds, how something so bizarre – and vile – was so readily accepted as rational) they could be rendered incapacitated by trauma to the limbs. For sure they'd find a way of moving but it would make them easier to contain and handle if their main means of locomotion were denied them.

Despite the gung-ho attitude of the military joker, these were still people we were discussing, American citizens. An executive order would be required before the green light was given to deliberately wound and maim. The President took a lot less time than any of us were expecting to issue it.

***

I'm wearing full combat gear, as is everyone else in the BearCat except Daniel. The stuff's so heavy and confining I feel that nothing in the world can get at me and it's a reassuring feeling. So to see him, dressed in nothing but his normal clothes, checked shirt over a white Tee, faded denim jeans and sneakers makes my stomach flip over yet again.

"Okay," Daniel says, "let's do this."

I have to resist the urge to reach out for him, to grab hold of him and stop him from doing this. It's not too late…

But he's already at the rear doors of the BearCat, alongside a soldier who's reaching out to the handle.

My breath mists up the visor of my helmet, I'm breathing so deeply, heart hammering.

The soldier pulls down on the handle and swings the door open. Bright light from outside floods the interior of the BearCat and I squint against it, putting my hand over my eyes and bumping against the visor of my helmet. As my eyes readjust, I see Daniel in silhouette, the light around him like a corona. He raises an arm to wave but before I can return the gesture he's gone, out of the vehicle and the soldier is swinging the door to again.

If this was a movie, the audience would be groaning at the cliché, that turn and wave *always* means that's the last time we'll see that character alive.

Worst thing is, that's exactly what's going to happen and I know it. Daniel's going to die.

At least I hope he is.

***

Once we'd secured enough research material the work could begin in earnest. Amongst many other remarkable things, the infected were incredibly strong. For everyone's safety they were kept sedated at all times (and knocked out completely whenever close contact was required) but the levels of anaesthesia required were many times in excess of what would be considered a normal dose for a human being.

The work was intense and intensive. Everyone was well aware of the pressure we were under – with every day that passed the numbers of the infected grew. Contrary to what pretty much every fictional account of a zombie (and yes, there I've done it – used the "Z" word) apocalypse would be like, communication, military and political infrastructures remained in place. Why would they not? Does anyone really think that contingency plans would not be in place?

The new infection was officially classified as a pandemic three days after the first reported cases. Its spread was exponential – as expected – but then the curve flattened out and plateaued. At that moment, it was approximated that just under half the world's population were infected. If nothing was done to stop the spread of the infection, there was no doubt that the numbers would steadily increase until everyone was infected.

With the change in proportions of infected to non-infected, the frequency of attacks diminished simply as a result of there being fewer – or no – uninfected for those already carrying the disease to attack. Cities, which contained the highest populations were virtual no-go areas now with entire populations infected. Those still free of disease lived out of town in rural areas, small towns. Within the cities, the zombies behaviour changed. With no fresh prey, they entered a hibernation-like state, eerily standing or sitting unmoving at the roadsides.

At first this was seen as a good thing, the most optimistic saw it as the end of the infection, that it had somehow run its natural course and was slowly dying out. The zombies weren't dying though, they were just waiting. The stasis was temporary, a resting phase. Our own forays onto the streets of Frederick resulted in exactly the same response as every other country attempting similar strategies (and which we watched recordings of online). Our presence was detected easily with an immediate 'reawakening' of the zombies leading to full on attacks.

Dying out of its own accord?

No such luck.

And so began the work of determining what exactly we were dealing with. Once we knew that we would have a better idea of how – if – we could do anything about it.

***

I shuffle back into the cabin of the BearCat alongside the driver. The soldier who'd let Daniel out takes up position beside the CROWS, primes the M240 machine gun on top of the vehicle ready for action. Just in case.

I watch Daniel slowly make his way past the front of the armoured car, striding purposefully. He makes his way over the grass, heading towards some swings and a roundabout that stand in the middle of the small park. He doesn't look at us at all as he passes by, not even a quick glance and part of me is hurt by this before I realise just how selfish the sentiment is. Still, as I watch him move away from us I keep hoping that he'll turn, allow one last moment of contact.

He doesn't.

"They're coming." The driver leans forward and points and yes, here they come – three from beyond the play area, two men and a woman shuffling towards Daniel, arms outstretched towards him, grasping, reaching out. Over to the left two more make their stumbling way forward. These are in a worse state of repair than the other group, one of them can only stretch out one of his arms, the other dangles uselessly at his side against a dark stain on his white shirt. Such is the journey I've been on, such is the place I now find myself in the thought that springs immediately to mind is that he would have made a good test subject, just having the one arm and all, much easier to handle...

Dear God, what have I become?

Daniel has reached the play area now, his last few steps he'd been trotting rather than walking and I know that this is a sign that he's scared. The composure and strong-mindedness he'd shown all the way through this, all the time since he made his decision is faltering now at the last and I find it unbearably heart-breaking. "Ah shit Danny... " I whisper under my breath, as he reaches the roundabout and turns to sit down on it.

He's now facing us but I know he's too far away to be able to see any detail through the reinforced glass of the windscreen. That doesn't stop me raising an arm, the gesture more than a wave, a salute to his courage.

The three infected reach him first.

***

It took just short of a month for us to identify the virus that had caused the plague. The usual suspects were ruled out fairly quickly, we soon discovered this wasn't a variant on the influenza virus, A, B or C, human *or* avian. I can still remember the feeling when we realised that what we were dealing with was a mutation of the Herpes virus – not so much anticlimactic as majorly WTF! There was no denying it though, 60,000 years after its last major mutation, the virus – henceforth to be known as HSV-3 – had done so, significantly enough for this to be regarded as a saltation, and become what could potentially be the end of life – *human* life at least – on Earth.

The further discovery that the virus specifically targeted cells in the pineal gland gave us an understanding of the behavioural changes in the infected. HSV-3 acted as an oncovirus, interfering with the cell division and repair processes in much the same way as the papilloma viruses 16 and 18 interfered with cell regulation on the cervical epithelium, the precursor to the development of cancer. Only it did so much more rapidly – instantaneously almost, within minutes of exposure. CT scans of our heavily sedated test subjects showed massive enlargement of the pineal gland, the disrupted cell cycles leading to hyperplasia – some of the glands we scanned were three times their expected size.

The increased inter-cranial pressure brought about by this enlargement would in itself be enough to cause the aggressive violent behaviour exhibited by the infected but its effect would be exacerbated by massively increased levels of Melatonin, conferring increased metabolic rates and levels of endurance and strength.

This much we could be certain of, could explain rationally and scientifically. More hypothetical was our opinion that the shutting down process exhibited by so many of the infected – at least until 'new blood' came their way – was also down to the increased secretion of the hormone by the enlarged gland. In effect, the infected are hibernating, shutting down metabolic processes not required there and then but ready to spring into life (and yes, I sense the irony of using *that* particular word) when necessary.

This increased 'robustness' of the infected would also explain why they are able to survive often dreadful trauma and injuries. The hypothesis would support the notion of the damaged area somehow being isolated from the rest of the body. The virus thinks only of its own existence. Isolation within the brain is all it requires, the body it inhabits merely a means of locomotion, a way to find food...

We'd observed that, as time went on, the attacks became less violent than when the outbreak first occurred. Perhaps some kind of an equilibrium has been reached – in the early stages spread of the contagion was the priority, now it appears the attacks are simply a means of obtaining food, even a hibernating body needs some sustenance. HSV-3 is transmitted by body fluid contact in the same way as its benign forms 1 and 2 are. The process by which that happens is more... intense.

How to kill an infected? Kill the virus. How to kill the virus? Destroy its home.

It was a grey November day when Marine Two touched down in our landing pad. Three months into the outbreak and with the most optimistic estimates putting the ratio of infected to non-infected at four to one, the President was here in person to discuss our options for a cure.

***

I want to look away from the attack but can't. Something tells me that I owe Daniel at least this, to be witness to his... sacrifice. And so I force myself to watch.

It seems to last forever but in reality is over in seconds. He raises his hands in a defensive gesture as his attackers reach him and I try to convince myself that this is not a sign that at the very last moment he has realised what is happening, what he is doing – and has changed his mind.

Whatever its motivation, it's a futile gesture anyway and the momentum of the running infected brings all of them down in a heap, Daniel at the bottom, pinned down by the weight of the zombies. I see their heads moving back and forth, side to side and even though I can't see clearly I know what they're doing.

The other two arrive but realise they're too late. One of the feeding zombies raises its head from the trough and snarls at them. They back off. Somehow, this behaviour is more disturbing than the mindless rage they'd shown during the earlier part of the outbreak. This is a sign of intelligence and reason at work, of communication. They've evolved, changed – and the knowledge of this is terrifying. Maybe all those 'alternative' beliefs are right, maybe the pineal gland *is* the home of the soul.

Feeding over, the three infected clamber to their feet and move slowly away from Daniel's body. They do not approach the BearCat even though they must be aware of our presence. To do so means instant death – something else they've learned.

I hear a click as the driver beside me presses the button on the stopwatch he holds in his hand. "Timing now," he says, unnecessarily.

We wait. And wait.

"Three minutes and counting," the driver tells me and only now do I release the tension that has been building within me for all of that time in a loud sigh.

Over three minutes and Daniel still hasn't moved.

This might even work.

***

The recording came to an end, the bar showing its progress reaching the right hand side of the screen. The parallel bars of the pause symbol reverted back to the triangle of play.

For a few moments the room was silent as the enormity of what we had just watched sunk in. A two minute recording of a man sat on a chair in an otherwise bare room. White plastered walls broken only by a large metal door and a window with metal bars obscuring the view through it. A minute into the recording, he gets up off the chair and wanders across to the window to look out of it. A knock on the door is heard followed almost immediately by the sound of a metal cover being slid to one side. The man at the window turns to look at the door, at the small opening in it now revealed and raises a hand to acknowledge whoever is stood on the other side.

He smiles as he waves.

"And this man was infected you say?" The President eventually said.

"Technically he still is," Professor Elsevier replied, "the virus is still present inside him but the antivirals we've developed seem to be working, keeping the *excesses* of the infection under control. These anti-virals are themselves viruses, ones that compete with the HSV-3 virus but which in themselves are benign. By competing with the Herpes virus they suppress its effects."

Not a cure then, but the next best thing. Enough to bring things under control until a cure could be developed – at least that was the proposal we were putting to the President.

"We can confirm, however, that the vaccine is 100% effective."

And so it was. We could now protect ourselves against the

virus, stop its spread. Yay for us. Except, of course, it was the most Pyrrhic of Pyrrhic victories. Yes, we could prevent the spread of the infection but stopping to consider what that actually meant rubbed off some of the shine.

You get bitten by a zombie, the good news is you stay dead.

A hard one to sell.

But an easier sell than what we did have planned. Chances were there'd never be a 'cure' for the virus. That's the thing about viruses – they can be treated but not cured. This was as good as we were going to get, a chance to bring it under control, a chance to rebuild.

And so we discussed options. Options as to how we got the antivirals into the infected.

***

We retrieve Daniel's body and it's then that I see the damage that's been done to him. In my years as a doctor I've seen worse of course but when it's someone you know, it's hard to distance yourself.

I confirm he's dead, managing – despite the torn flesh – to find a pulse, or rather the lack of one and he's put into a body-bag. Armed guards stand watch all through this but I know we're at no real risk.

As his body is lifted into the BearCat I think about the three infected who attacked him. Where they are now, how they're feeling. Will it even work?

Daniel's system was flooded with the vaccine and the antivirals, his blood was full of them. How to get them into the infected, that was what we'd discussed with the President for long, long hours.

Ultimately we'd decided on the most direct route of all.

It's not perfect but it's all we've got. The only alternative was to stand by and do nothing at all. Ten minutes ago we had Daniel, now we have three carriers of the treatment regime. Nature, or the version of nature we now have will take its course and its spread will be inevitable. A high percentage, if not all of the treated will ultimately become prey to the still infected. It's all about numbers, about shifting the balance. A tiny percentage of the carriers won't be killed when they're attacked, when they pass on the antivirals. Others may even escape attacks completely. Another tiny percentage probably but even that's a huge number when you're looking at the population of the world. From tiny acorns and all that – we have to start somewhere.

Plans are being developed to locate those populations still unaffected, get them vaccinated, build up a herd immunity. It's early days and it may all be wasted effort. Who knows?

Right now it's all we've got.

Inhuman Remains

By K.M. Hazel

1

Time to take out the trash, he thought, opening the back doors of his rusting Transit van with the joyful smile of a deluded saint.

The fever in his blood had cooled and bliss sang in his veins.

Had he been anywhere but the disused section of Broomwick cemetery in the small hours of a balmy Saturday morning, he might have whistled while he worked. Or perhaps warbled, in his curious falsetto, a selection of the advertising jingles the TV taught him. Instead, he kept a lid on his good mood and maintained the low-key approach his nocturnal activities called for. He had been the cemetery's caretaker for almost seven years now. He expected to complete his work without interference but remained mindful that his continued freedom depended on not drawing attention to himself. After all, mother had taught him well that good children are seldom seen and never heard.

He clambered into the van and began to remove what looked like a giant chrysalis. Silvery moonlight sparkled on the plastic drop-cloth he had used to wrap his leftovers. The body – like all bodies – seemed to have doubled in weight in the time it had been cooling.

His fingers slipped over the slick binding as he dragged his burden to the rear of the Transit. He almost regretted cutting off her breasts now that he needed something to hold onto.

Grunting with the effort, he threw the body to the ground.

Dust kicked up from the impact, catching the light like microscopic flares.

He grabbed a shovel and jumped down onto the body, his heavy boots cracking ribs and expelling whatever air remained in its lungs. The corpse's shoulders jerked upright. A gout of thick blood exploded from its nose, sticking to the plastic wrapping like dark treacle.

He grinned, pleased with himself. A little boy in pink Wellington boots, standing ankle deep in a puddle of dirty rainwater, looked back at him from the recesses of his mind. The pale, pinched face snapped to the side as a hand armoured by dozens of rings slapped a bleeding welt into its cheek.

He jumped off the body as if stung, raising the shovel in an involuntary gesture of self-defence.

"I'm sorry," he whispered as the shovel descended in his trembling hands to rest beside him.

He sighed as he looked at the woman in the transparent shroud.

"Don't worry," he said, his voice betraying a slight lisp. "You'll soon be able to rest easy. I have a plot already picked out for you. It's a beautiful spot. Best of all, you'll have your own tree. Of course, I can't promise that I'll visit often... "

The sight of her staring eyes – dead and glassy as the beady eyes of a soft toy – unnerved him. He thought he had closed her eyes along with the agonised gaping of her mouth. Now her lips yawned wide again, baring teeth that seemed intent on biting through the tight plastic wrapping. Her dead gaze fixed him with mute accusation. He knew that bodies could do puzzling things in the aftermath of death. Sometimes they even spoke to him.

He used the shovel to move her head to the side. More dark blood leaked from her mouth, smearing on the plastic sheet. Dismissing his nervousness, he leaned the shovel against the van then hefted the body over his shoulder. He jiggled the dead weight until it felt comfortable, then used the shovel like a walking stick as he set off for his favourite part of the cemetery.

He moved away from the access road with its crop of weeds poking through pockmarked asphalt, and weaved a path among weathered, lichen pocked tombstones, his sharp eyes accustomed to darkness. He trampled forgotten graves with no thought for those underfoot.

The dead were in a happy place, beyond his reach.

That was something else mother had taught him.

His trailing boot toppled a vase filled with desiccated flowers. Dead chrysanthemums crumbled to powder and drifted away on the cool breeze like the ash from the crematorium chimney on burning days.

At last he saw the sycamore tree near the north wall and quickened his pace. His breath came in harsh gasps as he struggled with the burden of tonight's special lady. Her name had been Kelly in civilian life - a methadone prescription found in her bag told its own sorry tale - but he would remember only her street persona, Jasmine. Her game face had grown a mask of shadows as she stepped from under the street-light to whisper her alias like aural foreplay.

The tombstone beneath the threadbare sycamore tree read:

HERE LIES HENRY JACKSON,

BELOVED FATHER AND HUSBAND,

CALLED BY GOD TO HIS IMMORTAL REST

ON THIS DAY JANUARY 14th 1927

"Company, Henry," he said, letting Jasmine's body fall from his shoulder into the hole he had scraped into the stony ground after the cemetery had closed for the day. A shallow grave to be sure, but deep enough to keep this dead whore in her place for an eternity of loveless nights. He had performed a dozen similar desecrations in this part of the cemetery alone in the last three months.

Working fast, already sluggish with post-coital fatigue, he covered the body with the cemetery's rich, dark earth then disguised the disturbed grave with a covering of leaves. Satisfied with his camouflage, he wiped the sweat from his brow and departed, spade over shoulder, for the caretaker's house near the main gate, his lonely home since the death of his mother.

Now he began to whistle, his lips forming notes without conscious thought. It would have surprised him to learn that the melody he trilled into an otherwise silent night was one mother had sung to him as a baby. The notes flew beyond consciousness. His oblivious mind had begun to replay the time he had spent with Jasmine. He heard nothing but her lingering screams.

2

A week passed before he felt the urge again.

His need made him careless. He returned home empty handed, blood boiling in his veins, his pounding head ready to explode.

As he parked the van, he touched his face and winced. His fingers came away stained red from four deep furrows some nameless streetwalker's fake red nails had gouged into his cheek seconds before she jumped from the van. She had fought like a wild animal. In the past his victims had seemed resigned to their fate, going to death with grudging acceptance. Soon the police would have his description, perhaps even the number of his van. "Fuck! Fuck! Fuck!" he yelled, using one of the forbidden words. What would become of him now? He jabbed the heel of his hand into the centre of the steering wheel, triggering a long, mournful blast from the horn.

The horn's grating tone, like a liberating shriek, seemed to relieve some of his tension. His hand fell from the wheel into his lap, cutting off the strident din.

From deep within the dark cemetery, something responded to the horn's calling.

That was no fading echo. It had sounded like a wounded beast bellowing in pain.

His chest tightened around his fluttering heart as he listened for a repeat of the sound.

It was not unusual for him to surprise horny teenagers in the cemetery or catch vandals desecrating graves. Perhaps the intruder was nothing more sinister than an abandoned pet. He had found his share of unwanted animals in his time on the job. Dogs and cats usually, tied in sacks or lashed to trees by desperate owners in places no mourners would ever visit.

No animal ever cries out in its death throes. Animals fear the attentions of the predator. But human beings cling to hope, even when experience would suggest that to do so is folly. When the sound came again, a plaintive, drawn out howl of anguish, his resurrected erection left him hopeful that another tryst, somewhere in the cemetery, had ended as anticlimactically as his own.

He turned the key in the ignition and floored the accelerator, heading for the ill-used access road that led to the oldest part of the decaying bone-yard.

The van's lights revealed nothing but crumbling stone, dead leaves, conspiratorial clumps of trees swaying at the edges of his vision.

Glimpsing movement to his left, he stood on the brakes.

He leapt from the van clutching the pickaxe handle he kept behind the seat for situations that required more force than diplomacy. His nerves tingled with wolfish excitement.

He raised a flashlight, stabbing its bright beam into the dark.

"Who's there?" he called out, trapping an angel with eyes like white stones in the circle of roving light.

Branches rustled in the dark, stirred by the cold wind.

He stepped off the road and began to move amongst the tombstones, working his way towards the back of the cemetery, his ears straining for the slightest sound.

"You can't hide from me all night," he cried, his gleeful voice emerging from a smile big enough to split his face.

Fallen leaves crunched somewhere behind him.

He whirled around, playing the torch beam in a wide arc over tombstones that looked like rotting teeth.

"You haven't committed any real crime yet," he shouted, stepping on the balls of his feet. "We don't have to bring the police into this if you agree to be sensible. Just tell me where you are."

He pulled up, the beam of the flashlight dropping down to illuminate a pile of freshly turned earth.

"Oh Jesus," he whispered.

He peered over the mound of dirt into the hole it bordered.

Jasmine's grave!

Empty now except for the remnants of her plastic burial sheet.

Someone had found her body.

Not the police though, that was the important thing. The place would be crawling with cops if they had been on to him.

He heard the engine of his van start up and spun towards the sound.

"Son of a bitch," he cursed.

He chased the van as it drove back up the access road towards the house.

Its engine whined and sputtered. The Transit moved in fits and starts, grinding its gears as if driven by a complete novice. The motor cut out completely after another hundred yards.

He heard the key turning in the ignition, sparking nothing in the engine. He ran even harder, closing on his prey with every step.

The engine kicked into renewed life as he sprinted to within touching distance of the van's back doors.

The Transit pulled away, weaving like a drunk in the middle of the road. He ran alongside the slow moving vehicle, pounding the driver's side door with the pickaxe handle.

"Stop the effing van!" he yelled.

A face turned with unnatural slowness to look at him through the grimy glass on the driver's side.

He felt his bladder let go as recognition spread over the face of the would-be thief.

Jasmine opened her mouth and screamed long and loud.

The sound that would have excited him beyond endurance at any other time.

Her eyes looked like bleached grapes pressed into the hard edged craters of her skull. Flaps of skin that had eluded the skinning knife sprouted comical tufts of blonde hair that offered a vivid contrast to the raw wound of her flayed scalp. Pus like bloody milk leaked from the wounds of her amputated breasts. He saw with glittering clarity maggots crawling in the hole in her tongue where he had ripped out her barbell piercing for his trophy collection. She was without question the most beautiful woman he had ever seen.

After what seemed an eternity, Jasmine's scream faded to a choking gurgle. She turned her head to look at the road, as though finally discounting him as a threat.

His acid-filled legs turned to rubber beneath him and he stumbled to his knees.

He tossed the flashlight after the van, his breath sawing in and out of his chest in ragged gulps as the torch flipped end over end. The van outran his missile, which broke apart on the road, and even managed to hold a straight line as it vanished in the darkness.

No way she could still be alive, his mind babbled, not after a week in the ground.

He had buried the bitch alive! What other explanation could there be?

He rose with every muscle trembling, fighting his body's urgent need to panic puke. He set off after the van, grateful to hear its engine cut-out again.

He found the Transit abandoned a quarter of a mile from the house. Right about now, he thought, she would be finding the main gate locked and the high cemetery walls too perilous to climb, surrounded as they were by abundant thorn bushes. It was just a matter of time before he ran her to ground.

He picked up one of the maggots crawling in the sprinkling of dirt Jasmine had left on the driver's seat. It writhed between finger and thumb as he examined it in the moonlight, its primitive brain driven by a blind instinct to survive.

The memory of his mother's bed sores punched the inside of his brain. Relatives of this pale squirming thing had eaten mother's dead flesh, carving the rot from her gangrenous wounds. They had been unable to save her legs though.

He squashed the maggot with his thumbnail, its rubbery body dying hard.

The sound of breaking glass made him gasp.

A deranged grin split his lean face.

She would find his home a trap, just as he had through all the long years of his childhood. Now he could enjoy the hunt.

At the rear of the house, he saw a window with a guillotine blade of fanged glass clinging to the top of the frame. Broken glass and splashes of blood covered the windowsill above the kitchen sink.

He used his key to gain entry and locked the door behind him.

He listened in darkness to the familiar sounds of the house: ticking clocks, the drone of his mother's old radio that would continue to play for as long as breath remained in his body.

"Ready or not, here I come," he said.

He turned on the light and put the pickaxe handle on the table.

Blood spots on the linoleum led to the hall door.

Taking the largest butcher knife from the rack on the wall, he followed the blood trail into the gloomy hall.

He darted into a sitting room on his left. He snapped on the light as he stepped inside, whirling with the knife to prevent a surprise attack.

The smart play would have been for her to call the police, but he doubted she was thinking straight in her condition. The only phone in the house was the one in the sitting room. The intact patina of dust covering its ancient Bakelite confirmed that no one had touched it in months. He cut the phone cord anyway. Better safe than sorry.

Leaping out into the long hallway, he spun around in empty darkness.

He switched on both hall and landing lights.

Dim bulbs flared into meagre radiance.

Blood guided him up the stairs. Tiny Rorschach spills on the bare wood teased associations from his mind that made his cock ache with the need for release.

"Might as well give yourself up," he called out as he edged along the first-floor landing, his voice echoing through the silent house. "There's nowhere in this house you can hide. No place I don't know about. Make it easy on yourself and you can get me now, while I'm still in a passable mood."

A long, inhuman wail resounded through the house.

He smiled, despite the hair on the back of his neck prickling as the last echoes of Jasmine's cry fell away.

She was on the third floor.

His hand groped around the edge of an open door and threw a light switch.

A bulb flickered with a sound like an angry wasp and then threw out a stable light.

He gazed up the steep flight of cramped stairs leading to the third floor.

Fresh footprints in the thick carpet of dust reminded him that he had not passed this way in the longest time.

137

He began to climb the stairs.

"Did you lose your mind down in the hole?"

Boards creaked underfoot as if in pain.

His fingers traced the grease mark on the wall, rising with him like a two-dimensional rail. Mother had rested her head on that spot during her long spells of delirium, wearing away the pale blue paint in a long snail track as she walked up and down the stairs, her demented peregrinations eating up days at a time.

"Well, there's no fixing you in that case. You might as well let me have at it. What do you say? Will you let me finish the job?"

He paused at the top of the stairs to gaze down the long corridor at the open door to mother's room.

Jasmine's scream erupted from the open door, startling him into dropping the knife.

The blade sank an inch into the floorboard beside his foot.

"I'm not afraid of you," he whispered, as though afraid someone else might hear. "You're not my mother."

He pulled the knife free with a grunt and moved towards the door.

"And I'm not your little boy anymore."

His hand tightened on the handle of the knife.

"I'm the man of the house."

He kicked the door to mother's room all the way open.

Jasmine sat in the dark on the edge of mother's bed, her back turned to him. Her breathing sounded liquid and consumptive. He watched the rise and fall of her shoulders and remembered times he had lain beside his mother in that bed. Watching her sleep with her eyes open, his child-self afraid to move, to betray himself with a breath snatched in fear...

Jasmine's shoulders stopped moving. Air no longer entered her body. Instead, what oxygen remained in her lungs escaped in an endless gasp from the leaking valve of her mouth. The habits of her old life no longer held sway.

Her head made a slow, jerky revolution. Above her shoulder her visible eye glowed like the luminescent dial of an old alarm clock. He felt his erection shrivel as she rose in a single jerking motion and began to move towards him.

She was wearing one of mother's old evening dresses, he now saw, one of the many treasured souvenirs of her youth. In place of the trophy he had cut from her head, Jasmine now wore one of mother's wigs. A platinum blonde Veronica Lake number that served to highlight the dirt and blood ingrained in her dead skin. Blood flowed like tears from her left eye, squeezed out by whatever moved inside the membranous sac of glowing ichor that still retained its ability to see.

Drake focused on the livid marks his fingers had left in her throat as Mother smiled from Jasmine's face.

She stinks, his mind shrieked, a stench no amount of stolen perfume could hope to disguise.

His tongue licked over dry lips as he gazed at her fulsome breasts. Mother's mastectomy prosthetics, he realised as his trembling hand reached out, eager to caress them. A terrible memory made him gag on the phantom taste of talcum-scented rubber. He snatched his hand back as if it had betrayed him.

For a moment, the spell cast by the wig and dress had been almost complete. He closed his eyes and wished the spectre away.

"Hungry," Jasmine said. *"Hungry."*

His eyes snapped open as she came for him.

Her hand came from behind her back brandishing a dagger of glass from the broken kitchen window. She raised the transparent blade over her head as she lurched towards him on stiff, uncoordinated legs. He could hear the rumbling of her stomach as she closed the distance between them in a sudden blur of motion.

He caught her wrist as the shard of glass arced towards his face.

His own blade slipped into her stomach, grating on bone as the backstroke set it free.

Her teeth snapped together an inch from his nose.

He stabbed the knife through her cheek and up into her soft palate.

Her free hand clawed at his eyes.

His precipitous backward momentum sent them sprawling onto the floor of the corridor.

Jasmine straddled him as she tried to force the shard of glass into his eye. The makeshift weapon had cut into the palm of her hand. Her blood dripped onto his face.

He snatched the knife from her cheek and plunged it into her belly.

She swatted the knife from his hand as if it were no more than a troublesome fly, sending it skittering over floorboards and through the open door of a disused bathroom.

He caught a whiff of her breath. *Jesus!* Like a ten year old turd wrapped in rotten meat.

"Hungry," she repeated, the truncated statement sounded

as weary as a deathbed confession.

"I effing killed you," Drake said in an awestruck whisper, the truth dawning on him at last. "So why aren't you dead?"

She dipped her head towards him. He remembered the way mother had bent over his bed in search of goodnight kisses.

"Huuuuuuuuungry."

His eyes snapped shut as he felt Jasmine's lips brush his cheek. He was hard again.

"No," he murmured, "please."

"Hungry," she reiterated, the delicious scent of him filling her nostrils.

Jasmine caught his upper lip between her teeth and yanked her head back. She ripped away the flap of skin beneath his nose along with part of his right cheek.

He screamed in agony as she devoured his flesh.

"Hungry," she said again, this time with more urgency, and bent her head to the feast. He raised his hand to stop her and she bit down hard on three of his fingers, shearing them off at the knuckles. She gulped them down, her throat bulging with the effort. Shock robbed him of his strength. He was unable to resist as the dagger of glass inched towards his left eye. The blunt point skewered the gelid sac on its way through his head, plunging into his brain before breaking on the back of his skull.

He saw a light.

Mother...

And screamed...

3

After she had finished feeding, Jasmine left her killer and staggered down the stairs, her steps unsteady in this new-born state.

It was as though her body were still trapped in sleep, not yet quite her own. Appetites turned her body into a chemical battleground, appetites she had never felt this keenly before. She glanced down at the track marks that threaded both bare arms and felt a wave of desperate need strike like a fist inside her bloated stomach.

She had to find her way home.

Home... *What did that even mean?*

She gazed at the home-made tattoo on her wrist, a crudely etched pentagram enclosing the letter B, and felt a stirring of memory. She remembered the man who had put it there, branding her like cattle with a permanent reminder that she belonged to him now, and that he would never, ever allow her to leave him.

4

Bonesteele sat naked and cross-legged in the dark of his squat. He listened to the distant wail of a police car as it chased down its quarry somewhere on the housing estate where he alone represented the rule of law to the tenants poverty condemned to live there. He smiled, exposing four glittering gold teeth, knowing he was untouchable.

His ebony skin glowed like polished mahogany by the light of six black candles. The candles marked the edges of a pentagram painted onto the bare floorboards. Inside the pentagram lay the body of a malnourished Caucasian baby that he had cut from the belly of one of his bitches as she languished in a heroin dream. A knife protruded from the chest of the infant. Blood had pooled beneath its tiny body, partially obscuring the magical lines of the pentagram.

He closed his eyes, resurrecting a face in his mind with crystal clarity.

"Come home," he whispered, "come home to me my lovely."

As if responding to Bonesteele's words, a sudden wind burst through the windows overlooking the car-park, extinguishing the candles around the pentagram as though sealing an unholy covenant.

Bonesteele rose and closed the windows. He peered through a pane smeared with window polish into the dark night, seeing nothing out there that pleased him.

Jasmine had been holding out on him according to the girl looking to step up and take her place. Keeping back a little of his money each night to finance her escape back to the small-town shit box she had once been glad to leave. Missing for over a week now, Bonesteele had finally accepted that Jasmine had run out on him, a transgression he could not allow to go unpunished. Tonight he had worked his magic, using the dark legacy of his Caribbean upbringing to bring Jasmine home, employing a spell so potent it would bring her back no matter how far she tried to run from him.

There was a knock at the door, a heavy pounding as remorseless as the beat of his dark heart. He rose to answer it, not caring that he was still naked. He plucked the knife from the baby's body as he moved to welcome back his favourite girl.

He opened the door without checking the peep-hole, supremely confident in the magic he had worked.

"Welcome home, my—"

The speech he had prepared died on his lips.

"Hungry," Jasmine said, holding out her arms to him, "*hungry.*"

The Night Before

By N.O.A. Rawle

They arrived at night, real night, not the darkness of day that the Northern hemisphere harbours throughout the winter months. Outside, temperatures plummeted way below zero but, with their flesh, there was no sense – no feeling. They had trudged miles barefooted, clad in rags, following Harlan's blood trail to the trap.

We hid in the chalet, shivering despite the roaring fire stoked in the grate. My belly was knotted with fear. We were the last bastion of a species on the verge of extinction. I touched my pocket, checking for the cyanide capsule, not daring to think what it meant.

"Better dead than *Zed*," Harlan had quipped as he'd handed them round.

We'd all pocketed them quickly, as if they'd poison us on touch.

"Hey Jake, just think of me as Father Christmas!" he winked as he checked out our sizeable weapon cache.

Harlan purported to be an expert as he'd apprenticed to a Voodoo king in New Orleans. I doubted he knew how to kill a zombie better than the next guy; he just had the gift of the gab. He sure had conviction though, holed up here with us.

Pine smoke permeated the cabin, no longer the smell of Yule, but of dread. I glanced across at Jessie who'd not stopped sobbing since our deadly rationing. She had taken it harder than me but who would've believed that being a street kid would turn out to be a blessing?

"You know Jake, I lost everything – my home, family and future all became – this." She gestured out to the frozen mountainside. "Why the hell was I vegan? I should have

144

eaten that shit and turned like the rest of them!"

Viral Inc's holiday campaign had been one hell of a success. They had it planned so that no nation was left unaffected over the holiday period, each with custom-made goodies, be it for Christmas, Hanukkah, Kwanza or whatever. The human race should have seen it coming, even the name implied it but no one took it seriously until the switch. The cakes and pastries, the sweets and drinks were all poisoned. Viral Inc was, indeed, just that. Those who remained became fodder; killed and eaten until every pocket of humanity had been lost.

"Here they come!" Harlan hollered.

I peered out into the moonlight. The northern lights painted the pristine snow a deathly pallor as they approached, shuffling and tumbling towards us, perhaps the last fresh meal they would taste.

I caught Jessie's nod, almost insignificant until I saw that more than half my compatriots were downing their capsules.

"Nooooo!!" Harlan screamed but it was too late.

Jessie changed first, her body twisting grotesquely as she contorted, the blank look of zombification gripping her.

"Harlan, what the—?"

He inspected the packet from which he'd popped the capsules into our palms. To our dismay, there in the foil was embossed the all too familiar Viral Inc corporate logo.

Zombie Girl at Five

By John Kujawski

She looked like a zombie, and everyone I knew wondered why I never asked her out. One Monday night, I reflected on this when I was out for my drive. I felt like I made the right choice not to date her.

I did like her appearance, though. She was beautiful. She was as pale as death, and that was something I adored. I used to see her at the cafe when I'd go in there late. They had her working hard. She'd be off in the corner sweeping the place up, and we'd usually make eye contact. She was thin like me, but I'd say she weighed considerably less. Her hair was dyed purple, and she was always wearing black.

I could remember the specific moment when I felt torn. When part of me wanted to have her in my life. It was around five in the evening, and it had been getting dark early. It was cold out, and I came to the cafe to grab a quick coffee. That girl was off in the corner with a broom in her hand, just sweeping away.

I was getting antsy in my seat. I was at my table, but I wanted to go talk to her. I just couldn't do it. The truth was, I had another woman in my life. She was the real deal, too. I felt like this girl at the cafe was trying to look a certain way. I liked it, but she was dead set on resembling a zombie. But that was the day I could have taken the first step towards meeting her.

The only steps I ended up taking were the ones that led me out the back door and off to my car. I had to get out of the place. I realised that girl was probably a bit like an actress. She had made herself into character of sorts, and I knew where I was needed that day.

I started driving away from the city and into the dark of the night. It took a while to get to where I needed to be. The thing was, the wait was worth it. I had something special in my life. I drove down to where the graves were, through the fog and cold air, until I stopped at my usual spot. At that point I just waited.

Off in the distance I could see her. She was coming out of the ground again, covered in dirt. She was near a gravestone. Her long black hair was all the way down her back, and she was the true vision of death that I had once again come to see. There was no way I could have dated the girl at the cafe.

How could I fall for a fake zombie when I was in love with a real one?

Zombie Baby

Into the Mouths of Babes

By Sheri White

This was Tammy's life now. Taking care of a baby that never slept; that was always hungry. She was his only source of nourishment; there was nobody to help her, to give her a desperately needed break. If he would stop crying for just a little while, she could take a nap and regroup. But he cried day and night, never satisfied with what Tammy could provide.

Tammy had given birth to Eric just four months before. Her husband Bill had helped her deliver in their bedroom; there were no doctors around anymore, no hospitals. The 'shufflers' had destroyed civilization as they knew it. There was a lot of denial when the dead started to rise. That only happened in movies, not in real life. Nobody would say the word 'zombie,' not even the President when he addressed the nation for the last time. Calling them zombies would validate their existence, and nobody was ready to do that.

She and Bill had prepared for the worst once it was obvious what was going on. Nobody knew how it started – was it a virus? A biological weapon gone wrong? There were no answers, and after a while it didn't matter. All that mattered was survival. So Tammy and Bill had stocked up on food, water, and emergency supplies, and locked themselves in their house. They also made sure they had a lot of birthing supplies, knowing that Tammy would be having the baby at home.

They thought they had prepared for every eventuality, but it never occurred to them that their baby would be born a shuffler. When Bill had pulled Eric out of her womb, his joy turned to horror when he saw the baby. Its skin was grey and mottled, his eyes dead white. At first Tammy thought he was dead; now she wished he had been. The cry that emerged from his mouth was inhuman, unholy. He was born toothless, of course, but had the common long, sharp fingernails of a newborn, and they scratched Bill, drawing blood, before he could react. He dropped the baby and grabbed his wrist, screaming in defeat. He knew what that scratch meant. One of the warnings the newscasts had offered was that even just a scratch would turn a human into a shuffler.

The baby landed on the soft bed, and Tammy snatched him up. She swaddled him in the bed sheets so he couldn't scratch her, and cradled him to her breast. Bill had been appalled, his wound momentarily forgotten as he watched his wife croon to their undead son.

"Tammy, we have to get rid of that *thing* before it kills you. Let me take it and leave; I don't have long before I turn. I don't want to hurt you."

"Bill, he's our *son*. We can't just get rid of our baby!" Bill looked at her as if the situation had snapped her mind. "Remember? We were going to name him Eric." She looked up at Bill and smiled with a new mother's serene glow.

Bill's expression fell, a single tear leaked from his eye. He reached down to take the undead baby from her arms, but Tammy screamed at him. "Leave my baby alone! Get out! You're a monster now!"

"Honey, please. He's not alive; he's a *shuffler*. I don't know how or why, but he is. You can't keep him, and I won't leave you alone here with him. He'll turn you, too. You still have a chance."

He tried to take the baby again, but Tammy pulled it closer to her. "You're not taking my baby. You may be dead, but he isn't. He's just a baby." Before Bill could react, Tammy grabbed the pistol Bill kept under the pillow and shot him in the head. He was dead before he hit the floor. Tammy knew he wouldn't get back up; they had been trained on how to put down the undead.

***

She had nourished Eric for the past few months with pieces of flesh from his father. After Tammy had recovered from the birth, she had moved Bill into their walk-in freezer. She would wear gardening gloves when she fed Eric his meal; he would eagerly gum and suck at the piece of his father until it was finally ingested. His diapers were foul; she had to fight from being sick when she changed him.

But the crying never stopped; he was only quiet when feeding. During his last feeding, a couple hours before, she noticed two blackened teeth erupting from his bloody gums.

He needed more than his father's dead tissue. She knew he needed fresh food and only she could provide it. She headed for his room, resigned to what needed to happen, her head more clear than it had been in months. She took him in her arms, and for the first time, offered him her bare breast. As he clamped down fervently, suckling her blood and chewing her flesh, Tammy threw her head back and screamed in painful ecstasy.

High Risk

By Sarah Doebereiner

Samantha lay stretched out on a hospital bed. Piles of warm blankets layered over her pressed her body down into the mattress. Even so, a lingering chill in the air pressed around the exposed places on her nose and cheeks. Samantha's gaze darted around the ceiling. The overhead lights were off, but in a hospital there was never complete darkness. Two thin rows of emergency lights illuminated the space above her head. Samantha rolled to one side. Her firm, rounded belly protruded enough to make the turn difficult. She placed a hand over her abdomen to help guide the weight. Her muscles ached with soreness from remaining stationary too long. They shouldn't have let her sleep on her back. Bedrest made Samantha lose track of time, but she should be nearing the seven month mark. All the books said it was better to lie on the left side to optimize blood flow.

A monitor beside the bed showed two waving lines. A number in the corner of the screen dipped; it flashed momentarily red when she turned. After she settled, the numbers rose until they maintained a solid green. The baby in Samantha's belly kicked. The woman groped around the head of the bed for her call button. She wanted to call out for a nurse, but her throat was dry. It hurt more than it should have from drifting off for a nap. Something sticky clung to the side of her lips and cheek. She touched it, but couldn't wipe it away.

Samantha breathed deeply. The little feet pressing against her ribcage moved slightly to accommodate the momentary lack of space. The room was sterile – barren. No flowers, cards, or visitors. Samantha tried to remember how long she had been in the hospital, but couldn't. The end of the world made little logistical details like that seem unimportant.

How long? Samantha wondered. She wasn't even showing when the world ended. Those days seemed a lifetime away.

153

Her boyfriend David asked her to marry him in the spring time. His knees shook so badly he hadn't been able to get up from the kneeling position he took to ask her. She had opted to sit down beside him on the wet grass. They held hands; his were sweaty. Samantha pushed the thoughts away. She shivered. Snow floated down from the sky across her window and obscured any sunlight. The lattice had enough coverage to suggest it had been quite a storm.

A few more moments of rummaging produced the call button. Samantha pressed it firmly until the button turned orange. The space outside her room remained dead quiet. You'd think a hospital would be a busy place during the end of the world. Most people hadn't survived long enough to need a doctor. They tried to explain it all to her after the fact – the process of corpsification. Samantha wasn't interested in understanding how it happened, or why. When she closed her eyes she could still see David sitting there in the grass. She didn't want to think of him wandering the streets, covered in blood, with his mouth gaping open.

A woman in isolation garb entered the room. Samantha studied her eyebrows carefully from their position over the surgical mask. It was Emily. She plucked her eyebrows too thin at the ends. The woman plucked them for so many years that they stopped growing in properly. Her eyebrows looked half-hazard – like a moulting bird.

"Morning Emily," Samantha cooed, "my throat."

"I know. You went in for minor surgery when you developed a clot in your leg. It's probably still numb," the woman explained.

"Again?" Samantha had been under the knife more times in the last month than in her entire pre-apocalyptic life. Her heart rate spiked. The baby rolled, as if annoyed by the sound. The motion calmed her anxiety.

"Wyatt will be in to talk to you soon," the nurse promised.

"Where is he?"

"New patients," Emily answered like they were speaking about the weather. Emily's eyes widened. It had been a long time since they found any other survivors.

"How many? Men or women? Where did they come from?" Samantha gossiped. Emily's eyes didn't squint into a smile. Her expression remained placid and calm. It was uncharacteristically serious of her.

"The doc will stop in soon," she said again. She paused. "If you need anything, just call me."

Samantha sighed. Protocol didn't mean anything now. There wasn't even a government, let alone HIPPA. Emily patted the top of Samantha's belly before she left the room. Samantha took another deep breath. The baby was so big now that he pressed her lungs up into her chest. Bile rose in the back of her throat. The heartburn alone was nauseating. Bed rest made it worse, and she kept throwing clots. It was only a matter of time before the risk to her health would outweigh an early delivery.

Samantha stretched. The world had shrunken so much. At first, there had been nothing beyond the barricades. Then, nothing beyond the hospital. Now, there was nothing beyond the edge of her bed. A physical therapist (who never even passed his medical exam) swore that if she did enough exercises, that she would be able to walk after delivery. She couldn't run though. Samantha loved the idea of that kind of freedom, but she feared it too. The world outside was full of gnashing teeth. The familiar places just beyond the perimeter fence were eating themselves alive.

Samantha forced air out of her nose and worked on some stretches. She picked up her left foot and held it in the air to the count of five. The muscle burned. They told her to slowly place it back on the bed, but the more reps she did the faster the leg seemed to drop. There wasn't enough staff to police her too often about it, but she did sincerely want to keep blood circulation normal.

After a few reps of leg lifts she rested while tensing her buttocks. David would have laughed at her for that. The OBGYN said that along with kegels would help strengthen the floor of her pelvic wall. She wasn't exactly sure what that meant, but Dr Diana said it would keep her from peeing a little when she sneezed. Dr Diana would have been proud that at least one of her patients made it. The survivors were: predominantly male, few women, less children, and no one over 40. Maybe that was because older and younger folks are more susceptible to infections and illness. Samantha shrugged. She watched the snow fall. When the baby got fussy she rocked her body gently from side to side until he fell asleep.

Footsteps outside her room drew her attention. They weren't Emily's light, somewhat malnourished prints. They were heavier, but sloppy. Samantha listened for the little shuffle that signalled Dr Wyatt. His apartment building caught fire during the riots, and he had been forced to jump out of a second story window. It still bothered him all these months later. Step – pause – scrape – step.

"Come on in, Wyatt," Samantha offered. She smiled at the doorway. Wyatt hovered. He paced around outside for a few moments in case she needed to collect herself. Samantha used the pad attached to the bed to raise her position slightly. When the grinding metal stopped, Wyatt entered. He wore the same papery covers and gloves that Emily had, but he always forgoed the mask. He said that in a world full of deranged corpsification, we should all try to make things a less frightening.

"Samantha."

Wyatt pulled a circular stool to the side of her bed. One of the three wheels on the stool stuck when it moved. It squeaked unbearably. If the world hadn't ended, he would have got a replacement, or he could have paid someone to fix it. It was little things like that, that reminded them how desperate their situation might become. Samantha noticed he didn't have her chart in his hands.

"Wyatt?"

"I think it's time to talk about delivery," he spoke. He looked over his shoulder towards the door. He kept his attention focused there. Excitement washed over Samantha. It was early, but not too early. They had all the equipment they would need in the NICU.

"I—" Samantha began, but Wyatt interrupted.

"First, I want to show you something," his words carried towards the door. Samantha shifted her focus from the back of his head. Emily reappeared with a wheelchair in tow. Months and months of waiting, and it was finally happening. Samantha tried to push down her fear. Could she raise a child alone, in a world of monstrosities? She thought of David. She could do it for him.

"I'm ready," she lied.

Wyatt lifted her into the wheelchair while Emily steadied it. The nurse pushed her so that Wyatt could walk alongside. The corridor of the hospital was in worse repair since the last time Samantha had seen it. Most of the windows were blocked off. The doors were closed, and the entryways covered in thick plastic. They rounded the nurse's station without seeing another person.

How many? Samantha asked herself. There were a hundred when she arrived. *How many of those survived?* It was hard enough to justify bringing a child into a world without experience, limited resources, and constant threat of danger. The thought of three individuals facing the end of the world was too much. *What if there is no chance of a real future?*

"We are leaving intensive care. It will be louder and busier than you are used to, so try to prepare yourself," Emily warned. The nurse's knuckles clenched the handles of the wheelchair so tightly that the bones jutted up towards the surface of her skin. The warning might have meant to caution Samantha, but in fact it soothed her growing anxiety of isolation. There *were* people beyond that door.

"Why are we leaving intensive care?" Samantha asked. Neither person answered.

Vast metal doors parted in front of them. Intensive care dumped out into a large open area. Samantha gasped. A crowd of people had amassed in the open space. Their deformities were so dominant that for a moment Samantha thought they were wheeling her into a nest of corpsified bodies.

The faces before her looked broken and uneven. Large chunks of flesh had been cut, or ripped away, and patched back together. Their bodies were scarred with old wounds. At least the freshest wounds were covered in bandages. When the faces saw her, they smiled – rather, they tried to smile with the sagging, somewhat lacking, facial features. Samantha tried to push herself backwards. Emily held the wheelchair firmly in place. She turned and smacked at the woman's hands. She couldn't be there. It wasn't safe for them.

"Sammy," A voice rose from the crowd. To her horror, it was a voice she recognized.

"Nette?" She spoke without looking back. The voice sounded like her sister, Annette, but that wasn't possible. She wouldn't have survived. Samantha wrapped her arms around her chest and squeezed until it hurt. It wasn't Nette, though she couldn't bring herself to check.

"I thought—" Wyatt said.

"Take us back! Get us out of here," Samantha ordered. Wyatt tried to reason with her. Emily withdrew towards the doors. Samantha covered her eyes. She didn't want to see them. When they reached the safety of intensive care Samantha could breathe again. Wyatt knelt in front of her. He winced when his injured leg touched the ground.

"Those people are not like you and me," he said. He cradled Samantha's face in his hands so that she was forced to look him in the eyes.

"They are monst—"

"Stop. Those people are not survivors. They are some of the thousands of people successfully treated for corpsification," he spoke the words gently. His touch lightened, and he released her. She resisted the urge to look away from him. Their eyes locked.

"Then, they found a treatment?" Samantha frowned. That would change everything.

"I did. I developed a treatment. Not everyone is a good candidate. If there is extensive brain damage, the subjects don't survive the – well – re-reanimation process. I need you to listen to me. Not everyone can come back. Do you understand that? We have to cut away the necrotized tissue. The living dead are just that. What was left underneath was alive and could flourish once we cleared out the contaminants," Wyatt explained.

His words were rushed such that he barely stopped to breathe. Samantha had no room to interject. Emily's hands touched her shoulders. The woman held her firmly, protectively even. *It's good news*, Samantha thought. *If they had just told me, prepared me I might not have reacted so insensitively.*

"This is amazing, isn't it?" Samantha asked.

"It is," Emily confirmed. She squeezed Samantha's shoulders.

"When they 'died', they rose again in a feral state." The living are carriers too, but the cells in the living hosts are inert and useless to build a vaccine. The cells in the corpsified are mutated from one individual to the next, meaning that a cure would have to be specialized from one individual to the next," Wyatt added.

"You cured each of those people one by one?" Samantha asked. Her eyes widened. She couldn't imagine Wyatt trapping corpsified humans with his gimp. Emily wasn't strong enough either. It was amazing. There was no other word for it, but that didn't explain why they were acting so oddly.

"No, I didn't," Wyatt admitted. "I just wanted you to see them, with your own eyes so you would understand."

"Understand what?" Samantha questioned. Wyatt's eyes looked dark and heavy. He squinted at her the expression on her face as though it pained him to look at her.

"I used embryonic cells from the blood of a corpsified fetus that was still being constantly infused with living blood. The cells were in a state of flux constantly trying to fight the corpsification," Wyatt paused.

"I'm so sorry, Sam," Emily spoke like Wyatt's words explained everything. The woman's voice pinched off. She wrapped her arms fully around Samantha's back. Droplets from her tears fell on the pregnant woman's shoulder.

"I don't understand what that means," Samantha shook her head. She touched her budging belly. When she pressed against the surface, the little body within moved in response. Her baby was alive. She could feel it inside her, alive.

"About a month ago, your baby died. The cord wrapped around its neck, nothing could have stopped it. I didn't even notice at first because the dormant infection in your body became active and reanimated it almost immediately. But Samantha, it isn't growing, isn't changing. The fetus has corpsified. Instead of infecting you, or killing you with sepsis, your bodies adapted to one another. You feed the infant healthy living cells, and it cannibalises them to survive," Wyatt finished.

"That doesn't make any sense. You couldn't keep that from me. You couldn't take blood and tissue from my daughter. Emily?" Samantha pushed her head to the side so that it butted into Emily's head. The woman hugged her tighter. She sobbed gently.

"Our research saved the world, but now it's time to talk about—"

"Delivery," Samantha remembered. She felt suddenly sick. She swallowed hard to push the feeling away. "My baby is a zombie?"

"No, Samantha. Listen carefully because it's important you understand. Your baby is not alive, but it's not undead. When we remove it, without your blood infusing it with life, it will die. Its body is constantly trying to fight the corpsification, but it will never be successful."

"You've helped so many people," Emily said. She withdrew from her place around Samantha's neck.

"David? Did you save David, too?" Samantha asked.

Wyatt shook his head. Once the treatment proved to be effective, they had tried to locate people from Samantha's past to make the transition easier. The corpsified didn't wander too far from their original habitat. So many had been outright destroyed that the odds of finding anyone were astronomical. It was dumb luck that they had stumbled on Annette.

"It's time," Wyatt said. It wasn't a question. There was no room for discussion.

"No," Samantha answered. It was too much, too soon. The baby in her belly rolled.

"Sam," Emily pleaded.

"No!"

"It will never be born," Wyatt reiterated.

"But it won't die either, will it?" Samantha guessed. She rubbed the top of her belly with her fingertips.

"I suppose not, but Samantha—"

"I refuse."

"Sam, you can't stay this way forever," Emily said.

"Actually, if I am understanding it correctly, that is the only thing I can do. You experimented on us. You took blood and cells from my daughter without my consent, and didn't even tell me when she died. You owe me this. Leave her with me," her words held a finality that disturbed Wyatt.

"You are a hero, your baby is a hero. Let it rest in peace," He argued.

"If you cut her out, against my will, history will remember you as *the monster* you really are."

***

Samantha sat in an antique rocking chair in a room painted white and pink. Nette and she had spent the better part of the previous afternoon on the second coat. Today, they planned to stencil teddy bears and horses around the perimeter. The paint fumes made her dizzy enough that she had taken a break while Nette went for lemonade.

Samantha's feet began to swell from the exertion, and it was barely ten in the morning. The gentle sway of her body sloshed her daughter forwards and back again. Little feet nudged the tight skin across her belly. The woman hummed lightly to the pristine nursery. Nothing was ever out of place, or worn, or used. Nothing ever would be.

Novocain

By John A DeMember

Gene cupped his hands over his son's ears; the moaning at the door sounded muffled to the young boy. The five-year-old could barely hear the deep, guttural sounds of the drooling monster merely feet away, its corroded fingers stabbing inarticulately at the door. The scrape of bone against wood effused the air like a sickly white-noise.

The boy's mother, Trish, with hands on her delicate hips, and her gaunt, birdlike form, looked like a decorative silhouette as she stood frozen in the hallway. The only light in the old, gutted house slipped from a gas lantern which rested on the edge of the imposing kitchen table. The grey light, a mote of cautious hope, jabbed dully at the surrounding darkness.

Like the last gasp of civilization, the solitary table stood defiantly; it was the only piece of wooden furniture her husband had spared from the axe. The winter had been long and unforgiving.

Trish begged him to leave the table, it was a family heirloom, but more importantly she needed something to hold on to, some sort of anchor to moor her to the life she once had, the life she hoped might magically reappear out of the rotting flesh and snapping jaws of the infected that had inherited her world.

"Bring him into the light Eugene," she said. "You're scaring him."

"He won't be a boy forever," Gene said. "He should get used to the sound so he doesn't panic when it counts."

Gene reluctantly let the boy go and gently ushered him to his mother. She took his tiny face into her hands and gave him a smile, the ritual was obviously long practiced between the two. She hugged the boy as he wiggled free and took up quietly playing with his toy cars on the kitchen floor.

"He's hungry," she said.

"I've been thinking," Gene said.

He joined his wife and son in the kitchen and produced a small black case, unzipped it, and placed its contents on the table – a syringe, vial, and various medical supplies.

"It's the only way, Trish," he said.

"What do you mean?" she said.

"I mean, we inject the Novocain into, let's say, my finger – cut it off, and—"

"Have you lost it?" she whispered. "I mean, there is no way—"

"It's not like I don't know the dosage!" he said.

"No!" she said. "Absolutely not!"

"That stupid thing is worthless now," he said pointing to a grey, rectangular spot on the wall where his dental degree once hung before he sacrificed the wood frame and paper for heat. "We do this," he said with sorrow in voice, "or we are all going to—"

"Don't you say it," Trish said sharply. "Don't fucking say that on front of him," she whispered, her eyes wandering to her son playing on the floor.

"Just one finger, Trish!" he said with desperation. "Just enough to keep him going for a bit."

"Has it come to this?" she said.

"It has," he said.

The moans outside grew in intensity as did the sounds of the skeletal digits scratching at the door. Trish carefully put her ear against one of the outside walls.

"Sounds like they are swarming out there again," Trish whispered. "I wonder what's setting them off."

"They can smell the death on us," Gene said.

Trish silently watched as Gene pulled up his shirt and unbuckled his belt. His pants nearly falling to the floor, he opened his pocket knife and stabbed another notch into the black leather. As he pulled his pants back up into place, he caught a glimpse of his pale white body; it looked sickly, sunken, and cadaverous. He pulled the belt impossibly tight against his phantom belly and looked back at his wife

"I should go check the windows and doors again," he said.

"One finger," she said.

"One finger," he repeated.

***

Weeks later, as another dawn broke free from its restraints and murdered night, the sun hung low in the sky, cautiously peaked out from the horizon, and gave birth to a cloud-riddled day more grey than the last.

Trish starred through a knot in one of the wooden planks covering the window, her mouth hung open in disbelief.

The front lawn, once green and palatial, now bile yellow and littered with the undead. Some stumbled along, their legs stabbed at the earth beneath them, their skin a steel grey and littered with coagulated sores. Some crawled, their arms hooked the ground as their bodies awkwardly inched along in the dirt, their entrails dragged behind them in a muck-soaked clump like an unwanted foetus. All of them eternally famished.

"Eugene, where are you?" she whispered. "There's more than usual out there."

A faint rustling could be heard from somewhere upstairs, but otherwise the home remained tomblike.

Trish trudged languidly down the long hallway amidst slivers of light which eked through tiny gaps in boarded windows and stabbed through the stygian darkness. Her gaunt hand, veined black against alabaster skin, gently stroked the wall as she spilled forward and up the stairs. Weak from hunger, it was all she could do to keep herself upright and moving.

"You guys up here?" she whispered and slowly opened the bedroom door.

Crouched over Eugene's nearly clad body, the young boy met his mother's wild gaze – bite marks riddled her husband's frail form, and the syringe dangled from his neck.

A string of bloody saliva swung from the boy's murder slick mouth. He continued to chew and, with an arch of his neck, the boy swallowed the flesh nearly whole. The ivory of Eugene's bones glistened amidst the jagged, torn flesh.

"What have you done?" Trish gasped.

As the bloody boy rose to his feet and pulled the half-empty syringe free, his father let out a final gurgle.

"More, mama," the boy said.

Starved, Trish lacked the strength to run.

Zombie Weird

Corps Cadavres

By Neil John Buchanan

Mayor shuffles in circles; his reins hang from his butchered mouth. His clothes have disintegrated, and his swollen legs have been reduced to black stumps. Doc sways in his saddle, gives a gentle sigh, and slips from his mount.

Doc is already half-turned. We can't have him go wild. Captain orders Mayor for dispatch, and Sarge steps up for the job.

Mayor looks to the middle distance with cataract eyes, oblivious to his impending 'second' death. Sarge unclips Mayor's head and without preamble removes his brain. Mayor looks confused as if he's just been told a joke he half-understands and pitches forward to lie dead in the dirt. Captain sets about the body with his 'taming' knife, stripping free skin with a practiced hand. When finished, he and Sarge roll Doc in fat so only his face can be seen. He looks like a giant maggot. The wild won't smell him that way.

Doc rambles about sex, filth, and the vanity of men. Towards the end, he talks of Bristol's heart and assures us its location.

On the Captain's command we each take a turn in stabbing Doc's face. He screams until blood runs down his throat. Captain's blade reaches deepest, and Doc stops moving.

When we're sure he's dead, we divide him amongst the troops. He won't come back this way.

It's what he would have wanted.

***

I ride a banker. His name is Sam. Obese in life, morbidly so, he makes good saddle. My legs fit into his, and I rest my head across his broad back. His swaying motion is soothing and sometimes I sleep. Not for long. Captain strikes my face with his yard stick; he points at his 'taming' knife and mimes eating my heart.

I don't sleep again.

The streets are filled with the wild. They clamber over each other in their hundreds, maybe their thousands. Pyramids of rotting flesh that rise into moonless skies. Sometimes the roads are filled with eyes, sometimes organs, or houses and towers of wet muscle.

Bristol is alive. Bristol is dead. And we... we are someplace in between.

In the endless procession of metal – humanity's last jam – the wild notice us.

It's Vicar's fault. He stumbles his ride, tripping Accountant's feet and slithers out her backside like a wayward child.

Vicar has chance to kill himself. His knife rests in its scabbard, one sure strike through the mouth and into the brain. He would remain pure. But he doesn't. Vicar is a coward. He deserves to die.

The men keep back, and the wild swarm in. They peel back Vicar's skin and sink hands into organs. Steam rises in thick clouds. They laugh, chortle, even snigger. Vicar has one eye removed, but the other looks at me, pleading. I lower my head in shame – what was I thinking – and urge my mount forward.

Sam wades through the wild, parting them with his huge hands. I press into his back, breathing his dried skin, and squirm inside his innards. The wild don't notice. When close I lean forward and use my knife to prevent Vicar from turning.

The wild busy themselves with pulling apart each

component piece. They separate skin from muscle, blood from veins. Organs are carried out like prize delicacies. Vicar's penis is held aloft like a gift from God. Nothing will go to waste. Vicar will serve Bristol.

My part is done. Sam returns to the troops, and we head into the Underground. Captain doesn't speak; he doesn't need to. I know he approves, can see the semblance of a smile before we enter the dark.

***

"Light your torches." Captain holds the burning stick aloft. We all follow suit.

My torch crackles and smells of bacon; grease runs down its wooden shaft and smears my fingers. I want to lick them, suck each one clean like they'd been dipped in honeysuckle.

Then I remember my torch was once McGregor, at least his rump. I can see the soft browns of his tattoo – a dragon winking at me as if sharing a secret joke.

I no longer want to lick my fingers.

Sam trembles. I pat his chins and coo in his ear to sooth him. He's a good mount; he has mileage, his obesity finding purpose in death it lacked in life. Not many could carry a man such long distances and still have legs to speak.

Rivers of blood wash through the tunnels in a raging torrent. The blood of a million lives, maybe more. Its warm spray catches me even from this distance, and I'm thankful for my mask.

Captain has us line up before the river. We know where it will lead; we were all there when Doc drew the maps. Captain doesn't need to explain. The choice came in the lowlands amongst the heather and machines, amongst relics and legends, back when there were twelve of us.

"There's no other way," Doc had said. "Bristol centre will

be a slab of heaving flesh. You have to take the tunnels."

Sarge finished turning the body on the spit. "If you're lying—"

"I'm not. Doc spat bloody phlegm into the fire. "I took sixty years to make it back to this God-forsaken island. This body is old, but my mind," he tapped the side of his head, "remains sharp."

Captain crossed to the fire. In its flickering light he looked god-like. He pulled a limb from the roast. "It's decided then. We leave at first light."

Now, Sam shies away from the river's edge. I yank on the reins, and we take the plunge. Despite my mask I taste iron; the blood is thick, not quite congealed. It flows in currents and eddies as we move downstream. Moments later we lose Jonah. His mount can't fight the current and goes down; Jonah goes with him. Only once – alive – do we see him, just his head and flailing arms, then he is gone into the dark. No one says anything. No one has to. By the time we make it to the next platform, Jonah is couched on the walkway. His head hangs to one side, his eyes roam the shadows. Captain orders lights out, and we float past.

Bedminster: all change. Sam is ruined; his limbs hang loose by his sides. His spine is cracked, and he has trouble standing. None of the other mounts have fared any better. Sarge calls for dispatch, and Captain agrees. The mounts' smell have been washed clean, their former stench cleansed in the rivers of blood. They are useless now.

I stroke Sam and whisper he did well. He mewls like a new-born kitten before I unclip his head box and remove his brain.

***

Temple Meads: last stop of the line. We find Prime where Doc said he would be.

Does he know what he caused? I doubt it, strapped to the gurney, even after all these years. His head has swollen, and his ribs have collapsed. He wears a suit leached of colour; a plastic poppy remains pinned to the lapel.

He moves at the sound of our approach; his teeth grind against the puckered hole of his mouth. I've seen pictures, loose pages handed around the farms, faces and people thought lost. Prime is a legend – the young considered a fable. He belongs to a different time so far removed to be beyond comprehension. Still, here he is, recognizable in death.

Captain hands over Doc's kit; he already fingers his knife. His eyes are wet, hungry. He knows. We all do. But we have to be certain.

"I trained to be a vet, you know." I unclip the saddlebag and remove the apparatus. "I've seen these devices used once before." I manage a smile. "And that was on a horse."

Captain doesn't respond, his attention on securing Temple Meads station from the wild. He has us move the gurney into a long-empty guard room. Blue veins creep across the floor like advancing weeds, and we do our best to avoid them.

Doc's kit isn't that complicated; I wind up a charge and run the tests. The needle sinks through necrotic tissue, and the lights switch from amber to red.

"What does it do?" Sarge inches closer, his eyes narrow as he views the device.

"We're all connected, right?"

Sarge gives a half-nod.

"Trust me, we are. Different sides of the same coin."

"I don't go into all that meta-hippy stuff."

I shrug. "It doesn't matter. Basically, this machine follows that connection. It can, in essence, tell us where we came from."

Sarge gives a small grunt. "I saw a car move once. They ran it on oil, made a hell of a noise, attracted the wild for miles."

"What was the point?"

"Culling, I think." Sarge rubs his hands. "People died."

"We have to start trusting in science. If this works, we could reclaim the cities."

Sarge's eyes find and hold mine. "That's how it started in the first place." He touches the apparatus. "How do we know it won't happen again?"

"Anything has to be better than this."

We lapse into silence, and a moment later the machine bleeps. I pull the needle free. "He's our man."

Captain gets busy cutting, while the others watch.

Before his heart is removed Prime asks, "Why?" His voice is weak, unused.

What can I say? You destroyed the old order; you ushered in a new age. You redefined what we knew about life. You robbed us of our dignity; you ensured world peace.

In the end I lean forward and whisper, "Reap what you have sown."

Captain lifts the heart clear. It continues to beat, although blood has long ceased to flow. The moment has a sense of importance. There should be speeches, music, clapping, even a drink or two. The whole world is watching. Instead the Captain slips the beating heart into his saddle bag, then hands it to me. "Not here," he points to the river. "It has to be taken beyond Bristol's limits. Sever the link and—"

The ground heaves and vomits rock. The walls shake. Brick, mortar and flesh slip free in an uneasy alliance, and the sound of a million shrieking wild echo across Bristol.

Sarge runs to the door. "Get ready," he says, licking his lips. "Here they come."

***

Thousands of wild swarm through the tunnels, perhaps more, summoned to the Prime's defence. They are a rolling tide of broken bodies, teeth, and groping hands. The ones at the back clamber across those at the front. They fill the tunnels, this sea of flesh, and spew guts, eyes, and bile into the guard room.

The soldiers do what they were trained to do. What they lived their lives to do. The air is filled with the slash of blades. A battle that is as fierce as it is short. No man can stand against such an enemy. The wild know no pain, and have no limitations. We stand upon a thin line between life and death; it takes but a second to cross.

It becomes a matter of numbers, and the men are dragged off to be peeled apart and used. Nothing wasted. Nothing lost. Not ever.

A grinding of metal and the roof sags. The guard room shifts as if shook by an invisible giant. Sarge is pulled into the wild. He keeps his 'taming' knife; perhaps he will remain pure?

Captain grabs metal rails, the hooks for archaic machinery, and I do the same. The floor gives way, and the wall becomes the roof. We hang by the rails and watch the wild squirm below us.

The roof breaks, sending showers of stone smashing past. Tendrils of fat slip down and hang as glistening white vines, eyeballs roll in their folds. Through the gaps I see stars and dark clouds. I'm reminded how very much I want to see another day.

Captain heaves himself into the rubble, using the fat as a makeshift ladder. After a moment's hesitation, I follow.

Outside, Bristol bucks and thrashes. No one else has made it, only the Captain and I. There's no place to run. Then we spy the centre. It's as Doc said, a gelatinous mass of flesh, alongside quivering buildings of muscle. Tending to it are a herd of wild. Giants in life, they tower above the others, slapping on fresh blood like the final pieces to a macabre jigsaw puzzle.

Captain pulls his knife, his chest is heaving, his armour stained with gore. "New mounts," his voice is barely above a whisper, but I hear him all the same.

I choose the largest, a small head on a body of lard. He's the easiest to bring down. Captain wards off the others, while I remove his jaw and pry open his skull. Once in, it's simple to detach sections of the frontal lobe: taking instincts, needs, and lasting desires.

"Done," I say slapping the skull back on like an oversized egg shell, but Captain doesn't answer.

He stands frozen in place, as if a mere statue of himself. Bristol has found him; its mind has reached out. I can hear its overflow: the jabber of millions. Captain has it all. He tries to speak, but can't. Instead, he looks to my new mount, then to the distant horizon. His grip tightens around his knife, and I salute him.

Captain forces the knife through his mouth and up into his brain. He remains pure. There is no shame in that. No shame.

***

I immerse myself in my mount's dark fluids, up to my neck in his filth. Bristol is a presence I cannot ignore, like cockroaches scrabbling at the walls of my mind. It has become sentient in a way that transcends the wild – truly greater than the sum of its parts. If I close my eyes I see it there: a black, singular point that grows in depth and intensity. It is a cancerous lump that devours all thought, reason and sanity.

It comes for me. It comes.

I dig in my heels and urge my mount to new speeds – but still Bristol follows – blocking out all else. I use my knife to cut a path through the wild. Cold hands slide across my back, fingers seek purchase. There are voices in my head. They promise pain.

Sarge appears from the masses. He grasps my arm and almost yanks me from my saddle.

A kick forces him back, and I urge my mount forward. Sarge goes down. His eyes find mine, his mouth shouting words I cannot hear. I will not hear. There can be no going back. I lower my head and ride on.

No shame. No shame.

Concrete and metal are replaced by hills and grass. The night gives way to day, and on the plains I ride my mount hard: great, lumbering strides that pass the miles. At our heels come the wild. They swarm from Bristol like ants in their millions, an army of seething figures with one singular purpose. Retrieve the heart. The further I go from Bristol, the weaker they become. My mount is susceptible. He staggers, and I'm forced to let him go, jumping from his flesh stirrups to continue on foot.

I gain the hills by mid-day. The fastest of the wild – thin, emaciated figures – catch me amongst the trees. But they are unsure of themselves, coming in small groups of two or three. They make too much noise, and I dispatch them with ease.

Bristol moves on the horizon: a vast, limitless construct

of flesh, blood and stone. It pulls itself from the earth, linked through spun flesh and monstrous ligaments. A head – the size of a mountain – emerges. Followed by shoulders, arms, a torso of broken metal, jagged glass, legs of twisting timber, concrete supports and iron pillars. Hundreds of eyes gleam from cavernous sockets, and search the wilderness. Its voice is the explosion of thunder; the tearing of the earth. A terrible unearthly cry. A birthing pain.

It's all I can do to just stand and watch, even the wild pause on the slopes below.

There can be no doubt. This is new life, born from the flesh of the dead. We're all connected, wasn't that what I told Sarge? Different sides of the same coin.

Bristol takes a step, a stride across miles. It screams: a long, unending blast of noise. Rivers of blood rush through its metal veins; concrete muscles flex, break and reform.

I have come far enough. There must be a divide between life and death. No more in-between. No more half-life. I take out my knife. Bristol falls silent, so many eyes upon me. I know what I should do. I know.

The world is watching.

Dolly Bone Dream

By Deborah Walker

Bone-house, cut-price dolly.

Desire is in your glazed, weak-tea eyes.

With your wire-thin arms, stretching out to touch me.

I close my mind to the wandering sounds,

the murmur of many mouths that speak your name.

You are not she.

The wind blows paper-thin skin into my face.

I cannot read your meaning.

This could be an end game.

This could be the fascination maybe-dream of

love longed for, and lost.

You are not she.

You are a naked necroscope,

viewed through my lens of prayer.

You are not she.

She is growing in God's acre.

And you, dolly-bone dream, are insensate facsimile.

You will burn away in some reality's flame.

Flesh and Blood

By Chris McGrane

Catherine and her faithful zombie Wormsmeat crept into the ale house at midnight. It was early spring, and she was in the mood to celebrate. The life of a ghoul gang leader was rarely a joyous one, no matter how vital her illicit skills might be in the modern economy.

The previous night her gang, the Harrowers, had defeated the White Skulls for control of Stone Fields, one of the largest burial sites in Dreadgate. Her long ascent, from street urchin to crime lord, had culminated with this victory, and wealth and power beckoned.

Ghoul gangs made a living illegally providing the resurrection factories with the corpses that they would then turn into the zombiefied workers that powered Britain's empire. While some corpse traders were legitimate and licenced by Parliament, many, like Catherine and her gang, operated outside the law. Competition for corpses was intense – demand for zombie workers had trebled by the mid-nineteenth century. Much of this demand was generated by the United States, the end of slavery motivated unscrupulous Southern land-owners to buy zombies to replace the slave labourers they had lost. Since the number of corpses that could legally be sold for resurrection each year was strictly limited[1], the Resurrection factories were often willing to pay illegal vendors large sums for the supply of additional

---

1   Under the Act for the Regulation of the Sale and Resurrection of Human Flesh and Blood, 1861, only certain kinds of corpses could be sold for resurrection – including those of convicted criminals, debtors who had died while insolvent, morphine addicts, suspected thaumaturges, mothers who had died while giving birth out of wedlock, soldiers or sailors who had deserted their posts and children or Irish people who had died without being initiated into the Protestant faith. Section 17 (subsections ii to ixi) of The Act made it a crime to convert other kinds of corpses (e.g. members of the Church of England, the landed gentry and published authors) into zombies. However, as demand for zombies increased in the mid-19th century, the intense competition for suitable corpses led some businesses to seek commercial advantage by illicitly procuring corpses that fell into the prohibited categories. To make these illegal purchases, and to maintain a degree of plausible deniability, the businesses often used third parties, known as Ghoul Gangs.
Southcott, M (1997). The Resurrection Industry: From 1650 to the Present. HUP. Hexford.

corpses. The ghoul gangs fought vicious battles with each other for control of graveyards, mortuaries, and other locations where corpses could be harvested.

Catherine had a long association with Chadwick's. As a youth, she had picked pockets here, before being recruited into the Harrowers. Catherine had even heard of the murder of her estranged mother, Evangeline, while the Harrowers were drunkenly celebrating some event at Chadwick's.

Evangeline died owing almost five thousand sovereigns. In an effort to recoup their expenses, the debtors had her corpse sold for resurrection. This resurrection was not the one promised by the Church whose services Catherine had so infrequently attended as a child. This was a purely physical restoration, achieved by administering a serum to a body, which then rose up, incapable of thought or speech, suited only to manual labour.

Three days later, her mother's resurrected corpse was purchased by Chadwick's alehouse, to perform menial chores.

Every evening, after a day of larceny, the young Catherine would come to the alehouse to watch her mother work. Someday, she would promise herself, she would be rich enough to buy the corpse and give it a decent burial. Yet, years later, now that the Battle of Stone Field had made her wealthy, Catherine couldn't bring herself to make the purchase.
The gang members roared in celebration and drank a toast. "To our Queen, Catherine, long may she reign."

Catherine celebrated long into the night and long after her fellows had gone home or passed out. As dawn came, she left the ale house. Her mother didn't react, and continued to clean as her only child stepped out into the cold, alone and unnoticed.

The next night, Catherine once again sat in Chadwick's ale house, watching her mother. The sepulchral figure was mopping the floor when she yelped, apparently surprised by a be-suited gentleman, who was walking past her toward the bar. Unused to seeing the zombie respond to a human presence, let alone display emotion, Catherine looked up from her ale. The stranger wore a small gold escutcheon on his lapel – inscribed on it was a sigil she did not recognise.

As the suited man came closer to the Evangeline's corpse, the death-marked face began to tense, and then the dead woman began to scream. She flailed her stone-cold limbs in panic and ran, howling like a damned soul. Old Chadwick ordered the zombie to heel, yet she ignored him, slashing his face with rock-hard fingers, sending the old man crashing to the ground. The man with the sigil drew a blade and attacked her, yet she dodged the blow with surprising grace and smashed in his skull with her grave-hardened hands.

With brutal grace, the huge enforcer who guarded the ale house door raised his cudgel, preparing to strike at the slender woman in the black dress. Rogue zombies – those who went wild and attacked their masters – were feared throughout the empire. Royal edict demanded they be terminated at the earliest opportunity.

From her chair near the door, Catherine drew her dark-metal revolver and fired, catching the enforcer in the shoulder. He dropped his cudgel and abandoned his ambush. Her mother ran through the front door and escaped the ale house.

Two more of Chadwick's men pursued the zombie, determined to retrieve their master's property, or destroy it. Catherine shot one in the kneecap, raising her gun to the other's sweaty red face.

"Piss off, mate," she said, holding the gun in one hand and taking the man's bowler hat and trying it on with her other.

"Outta my way. That Clay person[2] just went rogue, love. Law says we have to destroy it."

"Law also says no dice games, demimondaines, or smuggled goods – but I see lotsa them here."

"Some laws was made to be broken. But we takes the Rogue Zombie Laws seriously round 'ere." More thugs joined him. "Move along, my desert rose, or we'll pluck you where you stand," The leader snarled. She broke his knee with a savage kick, then summoned reinforcements of her own. Wormsmeat, who had crept into the ale-house to defend his mistress, began to growl and hiss. The enforcers reeled in horror. A feral zombie, unlike the tame domesticated ones, always inspired dread.

"Wormsmeat don't like seein' people threaten me. So I suggest you back down before he starts biting."

"Is he carrying the plague[3]?" one asked, clutching a protective holy symbol so tightly that his knuckles turned white from the effort.

"Attack me and you'll find out."

The enforcers retreated.

"You're insane," one man yelled. "Protecting rogue zombies – you'll hang for this."

Catherine smirked. "Plenty of people want to hang me, mate. But as I'm Queen of the largest and most vicious ghoul gang in Dreadgate, no one should risk upsettin' me, 'specially not a bunch of two-bit crooks like you." As the thugs cowered, Catherine and her zombie exited the

---

2   Zombies were often referred to as 'Clay people' in honour of US politician Henry Clay, one of the fathers of the international zombie trade, who espoused the creation of and use of undead workers as an alternative to slavery. Clay claimed that the introduction of zombie labourers into the Southern US states was a crucial reform that eventually allowed for the peaceful abolition of slavery and, so he claimed, allowed the US to avoid a bloody civil war on the issue. See 'Clay's Last Compromise.'
3   A reference to the zombie plagues or 'Creeping death' that had periodically terrorised Europe between 1200 and 1890.

building. She ruffled Wormsmeat's hair and offered him a scrap of marchpane as a treat. It had been her idea to have the zombie pretend to be plague-ridden, so as to scare her rivals, yet never before had she seen a zombie carry out a charade with such aplomb.

"Who were you before they zombified you, my dear?" she wondered.

The man with the sigil lay dead on the floor of the ale house. By the time they exited Chadwick's, Evangeline had vanished.

***

The debtor's prison in Dreadgate was not a welcoming place, yet Catherine visited often. Dame Evangeline D'Ark, had won fame as an explorer and later as one of the band of Parliamentary reformers who sought to abolish the zombie trade. Politics and exploration were expensive hobbies and Evangeline's small inheritance had been insufficient to bear the costs for long. Soon Dame Evangeline was deeply in debt and mired in scandal[4]. Her opponents in the zombie industry and the political establishment had her declared bankrupt, expelled from Parliament, and thrown into a debtor's prison. Catherine D'Ark, her only child, was consigned to an orphanage, from which she soon fled.

Catherine, who by seventeen was a veteran of numerous gang land battles, who had fought zombies, criminals, and the authorities without fear, still felt trepidation when asking a favour of her estranged mother. Life had not taught Catherine to respect tradition, yet there was one custom she felt unable to ignore. Victor was unlike most of the men she had met, he was by birth a Genovese, and his family was one of the most distinguished of that republic, yet her past did not trouble him. Having not yet reached her majority, Catherine would need her mother's permission in order to

---

4   Dame Evangeline's out of wedlock pregnancy scandalised London society – as did the fact that she gave birth to a child of mixed race.

marry him.

"You can't be seen with him, much less marry him. He isn't... suitable."

"Mother, you are the last person who can lecture me on respectability or propriety," Catherine said, sharply.

"He is deeply involved in the corpse trade – a trade I have spent my life opposing. I won't have a daughter of mine involved in such abominations."

"I admit the corpse trade is unpleasant, but for some, it is the only alternative to starvation. He is the man I will marry. If you don't give me your permission today, I will wait until I no longer require it."

"As you wish, dearest," She responded icily and fell silent. To a casual observer, it seemed to be a capitulation, yet Catherine knew it was merely the start of a long campaign of attrition.

They never argued, never screamed or shouted. That is not how aristocrats, even the fallen ones, behaved. Instead, silence settled between them like a heavy winter snow – killing everything beneath it.

Silence had been her mother's constant companion on her solo explorations, and it was silence that returned with her from these expeditions, like an unwanted guest in their home. As she grew older, Catherine found that, increasingly, silence greeted each and every question she posed to her mother. It was a cancer that spread into every aspect of their relationship.

After two hours, during which they did not utter a single word to each other, she left her mother's side, eyes stinging with tears.

Catherine spoke first, ordinarily an admission of defeat in their many silent contests of will.

"Remind me why you prefer silence, mother. I've told you about the man I love and wish to marry, I want your blessing. Why stay silent?"

"Sometimes silence is the only answer that seems truthful."

Catherine hissed, "Then if you ever ask me whether I love my mother or for my fondest memories of you, I'm sure you'll be able to understand the silence that follows your question."

Catherine stormed out of the prison and wished the old crone dead. Twelve hours later, her wish came true.
She broke off the engagement the same day.

***

The inn at All Harrow's Gate was the de facto throne-room of Catherine's criminal empire. Today, as usual her ghouls (a term that refers to undead and also to the armed human criminals who work in the grave robbing trade) guarded the entrance.

Dr Witch was a rogue theologian from Whitechapel whose experiments with the undead brought him to the attention of the authorities. In other eras he would have been burned at the stake, but nowadays, with the zombie trade becoming a lucrative business, the Resurrection factories were always looking to recruit new talent. While respectable firms would not publicly associate with the likes of Dr Witch, they covertly funded his illegal research – research aimed at finding newer, cheaper ways to re-animate the dead. The need for illicit flesh and blood had brought Dr Witch into contact with Catherine and her ghoul gang. Today, it was Catherine who needed his expertise.

Madame D'Ark told the doctor about the man with the sigil, who had scared her zombified mother and caused her to flee in panic.

"Could it be a sign? Some residual memory? A clue to her

murder?"

The doctor shrugged. "Re-animated corpses are little more than animals, easily scared by loud noises or unfamiliar things."

She drew the sigil on a tablecloth. "I have never seen this sigil before. Whose is it?"

The man crossed himself. "The sigil the Black Rat."

Even a whispered mention of the Black Rat was enough to silence the room. Centuries ago, when zombie-making was in its infancy, the Brotherhood of the Black Rat had been amongst the first to make the dead walk. Though reviled for this dark wonder, they were protected by both Church and Crown[5]. So The Black Rats became official court magicians – until they brought the zombie plague to London.

Some said this was deliberate, that the Black Rats worshipped the plague and sought to bring it to new lands, like missionaries of death. Others said the release of the plague was an accidental by-product of their resurrection technique. Regardless of their motive, their organisation was proscribed, their members exiled or burned alive. William the Black, leader of the Brotherhood, was hung, drawn and quartered on the personal command of Elizabeth I.

After she had roused them from their shocked silence, Catherine sent her troops in search of the Black Rat corpse from Chadwick's. An informer soon revealed that the Black Rat's body was taken to a local burial ground known as the Doomsday House[6].

"We have to raid it, acquire the body and dredge the brain for residual memories."

"That may not be possible My Lady," Dr Witch demurred.

---

5   Dr Dee, Queen Elizabeth I's personal astrologer, was said to be an admirer of the Brotherhood's early work.
6   Possibly a reference to the Gravedigger in Hamlet, Act 5, Scene 1, "The houses that he makes last till doomsday."

"Are you not the finest metaphysician in Dreadgate? Can't you dredge a dead brain for memories?"

"I can. But the graveyard you seek to raid is controlled by the Apostate Angels. A vicious ghoul gang – more ghoul than human – and not likely to share their bounty with anyone."

"Then we shall take that bounty by force. Mr. Stalker, summon all of my ghouls, and have them prepare for war."

***

In the aftermath of the raid, wounded gang members lay on the floor of All Harrow's Gate Inn. Dr Witch used his skills, both mundane and thaumaturgic to repair what damage he could. Catherine watched him reattach Scarlett Will's severed thumb and smiled in gratitude and wonder. Yet Witch and his fellow flesh mechanics could only repair so much damage. Twelve bodies lay on the floor. Catherine ordered their cremation. It was unthinkable for a ghoul gang to sell the corpses of its members.

Stalker was the oldest and toughest of her gang. He was one of the few who had been at her side from the very beginning through to their glorious victory at the Battle of Stone Field. She had been an upstart in Obsidian Steel Armour, who had dared challenge the city's most powerful ghoul gang for control of the field. By consistently poaching corpses buried on their territory, she had goaded them into assembling their forces in one place. Once they assembled in one place, she ambushed and defeated their entire underworld army. The next morning, all of the other gangs recognised her as the rightful ruler of the Stone Fields.

Stalker approached his Queen.

"The lads is worried, milady. Worried this business with your mother is affecting your judgement. Our latest grave raid, we lost a dozen ghouls, for the sake of a single corpse..."

Catherine greeted him with silence.

He continued nervously, "They is worried about being dragged into a war for the sake of a long dead woman."

Catherine responded, "This isn't about my mother. It is about survival."

"You sure, Milady?"

She reached for her gun. Beside her, Wormsmeat issued a low, menacing growl. "Do you doubt my judgement, Mr. Stalker?"

"No Milady."

"Good." She relaxed her grip on the gun. "My mother is dead to me. She had been for years – even before she was killed. I don't give a ghoul-shit what happened to her or why. But if the Brotherhood of the Black Rat has returned to this Sceptred Isle, then they could turn every corpse in the country into a walking plague carrier. And that would destroy a lot more than the corpse trade. The corpse we recovered was vital. We had to get to it before the Black Rat could destroy or resurrect it. Now that we have it, Dr Witch can search the brain for trace memories. Those memories should lead us to the Brotherhood. I'm protecting our business and our profit margin. Nothing more. I expect you to inform the troops of this, Mr Stalker."

He bowed. "As you wish, Milady."

As Stalker left, Catherine returned her gaze to portrait of her mother that hung on the wall of her chamber. She stared for a long time before she seized the portrait and smashed it furiously against the floor. She then stormed out of the inn. Wormsmeat followed behind her, a pensive look on his face.

***

Dr Witch extracted memories from the corpse of the Black Rat. The severed memories floated in the air in a weird smoke, which Catherine and her doctor inhaled. She felt a burst of nausea as the alien memories, not fruits of her own brain but from the mind of her foe, untimely ripped, seeping into her consciousness.

She saw her mother in the debtor's prison, speaking to an employee of the Resurgam Institute, one of the largest Resurrection factories in the world. He was telling her that the factory was breaking the law, using a version of the zombie plague to expedite the zombie creation process[7]. Evangeline smiled, here was the revelation that would doom the zombie trade. She opened a heart-shaped silver locket that held a portrait of her daughter. "I will create a better world for you, my dear child," she said.

Catherine lost sight of the memories for several moments, as her own emotions stirred and her tears made a blurry mess of the images. By the time Catherine could concentrate again, the memories had changed and showed the Black Rat, who had entered the cell under a false pretext, strangling Evangeline and leaving her corpse to fall onto the floor. He took the locket as a macabre souvenir and fled.

Eyes stinging with pain, Catherine exited the memory haze. Dr Witch, still inhaling and interpreting the memories, drew a detailed plan of the Resurgam Institute, one that included the Black Rat nest that nestled at its heart. He made an annotation in one of the cells used to restrain newly created zombies: Evangeline D'Ark.

***

She had spent days pouring over the map Dr Witch had drawn from the memory of the Black Rat. She had formed her ghouls into raiding parties and given detailed instructions to the party leaders. She had memorised the pass codes and passages she would need to take. It would be her most audacious raid yet. She would steal the recently

7   Ever since the zombie plague almost destroyed London in the 17th century, England had introduced a series of harsh laws aimed at preventing its return.

recovered heart of the Brotherhood's founder and exchange it for her mother... or what was left of her.

She had just changed into her raiding clothes – flight leather breeches, boots and a tunic, covered by an obsidian steel breastplate, when Dr Witch re-entered the inn. He'd been smoking morphine again. It was his preferred way to deal with the pain caused by subsuming another person's memories. His eyes turned midnight black as the drug took effect.

"They say things get easier with practice, so why is it so hard for you to abandon your mother to her death? You've done it before, you're well versed at it, so why can't you do it THIS time?"

"SILENCE," she screamed.

"Yes. Silence. That is the reason, isn't it? The icy silence between you and your mother. Do you aim to break it now? Years after her death?" He began to babble. Catherine, face reddening with rage, summoned two burly enforcers to remove him from her presence. "Can you channel the flame that burns inside you, forge a chain of loving deeds, louder than your hateful words? They say people bargain with death after a loved one dies. Is this your bargain? If you save your mother now, what little is left of her, will she hear you through the silence of death? Will it make amends?"

"Take him away, before I slit his throat!" she screamed. As he was dragged away, the morphine fever abated for a few moments.

"If her hell is made of silence, a word from you can save her."

Catherine finished her preparations, and she and her troops departed for the Resurrection factory, in complete silence.

***

Catherine and Wormsmeat stole through the desecrated church, moving as quickly and quietly as the shadows that once danced there during candle-lit vigils. The church was one of many buildings that had been repurposed as zombie creation facilities[8] during the reign of the Great Protector. Yet the building seemed to resist its new purpose, its myriad dark corners, altars and confessional booths providing hiding places for those who had no place in the new system. Making expert use of such camouflage, the fugitive pair had infiltrated the Resurrection Factory, stolen materials key to the owner's dark designs and made their way to the factory's core, a place that had once been the Cathedral's crypt.

The factory ultimately belonged to The Brotherhood of the Black Rat, a group that would not take kindly to the news that their messiah's heart had been stolen from the reliquary on the eve of his return. In a way, Catherine almost admired them. They created the entire modern zombie industry – with all its factories, research institutes and zombie production facilities, reshaped the whole of Europe, solely to perfect their art – and resurrect one man.

Catherine had reached the core before Black Rat, the cult leader and his forces found her.

"Where's my flesh and blood?" he demanded.

It was a common expression in the corpse trade. 'Flesh and Blood' referred to any intact corpse that was suitable for transformation into a zombie. The newly minted zombies would be sold for a profit to employers weary of their human workforce (and their constant demands for decent wages and conditions). She had sold many corpses to the Resurrection factories. Today, however, she would drive a bargain that would win her renown, or an untimely end.

---

8   As the word 'zombie' had negative connotations, the owners preferred to call such facilities 'Resurrection Factories.'

"The Founder's heart is in this bag," she said, holding up a hessian sack. "Now, where's *my* flesh and blood?"

Black Rat smiled enigmatically. "Your mother is here, safe with us. I wager you've been searching for her for a long time. When did she escape?"

"On the ninth of spring this year. Exactly three years after she was murdered."

***

Deep inside the Resurrection factory, Catherine D'Ark faced the leader of the Black Rat cult. Alarms sounded throughout the deconsecrated church, as her ghouls fought a savage battle with the cult members. Female members of her gang howled like Rose women[9] as they fought. She held the heart of William the Black and stepped closer to the open door of one of the massive coal furnaces that powered the factory.

"I can incinerate your founder's heart with one flick of my wrist," she warned. "Now bring my mother to me."

The cult leader obeyed. Her zombified mother soon stood next to her, hissing in fear at her captors.

Black Rat smiled. "Zombies are remarkable creatures, humanity's first tangible proof that life can continue beyond physical death – and all the reformers want to do is destroy them."

"Is that why you had my mother murdered? To ensure the zombie industry would survive?"

"Your mother wasn't supposed to die. Brother Silas was instructed to buy her silence, but she would not be bribed

---

9   One particular iteration of the zombie plague chiefly affected women and caused the infected to howl like Banshees. As this version of the plague caused red, rose-like blotches to bloom on the subjects' skin, infected were dubbed 'Rose women.' For a well-researched account of this plague, see Harlen's 1993 history *A Plague of Roses.* For a rather less credible account, watch Hans Kohl's 2001 movie *Night of the Killer Women!!!*

and he overreacted. You should thank me, I brought your mother into my laboratory and I gave her new life."

"How can you call this travesty 'life'?"

"You don't believe your mother is alive?"

"No."

"Then why fight to protect her? Chadwick's boys were going to destroy her. You stopped them. Why? Why would you risk your life, and those of your troops, unless you think that somewhere inside that shell some part of her is still alive? You KNOW she is still alive... don't pretend otherwise. Others may not appreciate our achievements, but I know you do."

"You're using the zombie plague to generate your undead workers. You've sold thousands of zombies, tainted by the plague. You could kill millions... "

"Many will die," He conceded. "But the worthy will rise again. The resurrection of our Founder will trigger the plague and destroy the sin and depravity of this world. Now give me back the Founder's heart, that we may restore him to life, and restore hope to the world."

Catherine was about to refuse when her mother, death-quick and bursting with unnatural vitality, seized the severed heart and grabbed her daughter by the throat. Wormsmeat sprang to his mistress' defence but Black Rat fired three shots from his revolver, and the faithful zombie fell.

The preternaturally strong woman squeezed, slowly choking her daughter with one hand, holding the severed heart of the founder in the other.

"You see? Your mother is a believer. Our faith offers her a chance to escape the flames of hell. But our faith is not for you... I am afraid there is no place for ghoul gangs in our new world. Any last words, Miss D'Ark?"

"I believe my mother is still alive."

"So do I."

"That's why I wanted her to have the honour."

"What honour?"

The old woman crushed the heart of William the Black, smashing it into a pulp on the stone floor. Black Rat screamed in pain. Wormsmeat, stunned by the bullet wounds, but not dead[10], rose and leapt upon the Black Rat. Enraged, the cult leader fired, not at the faithful zombie, but at the women who were the architects of his agony. The old woman pushed her daughter out of harm's way, absorbing the full brunt of the attack. As Black Rat fell, a bullet crushed the old woman's skull. Whatever light shone in those eyes blazed for a few brief moments, trying to defy an inevitable extinction. In trying to postpone her inevitable death, the zombie seemed more human than ever. Catherine wrapped her arms around her mother's frail form.

"You mean the world to me," she whispered. "You always have."

Catherine continued to speak, with a clumsiness borne of extreme emotion. It was a random, almost nonsensical outpouring of impassioned statements and declarations of love. As the old woman's eyes closed, Catherine had an impression of her mother's soul fleeing the hell to which she had consigned herself, and, guided by the sound of her daughter's voice, founding a path out of the dark.

"Catherine," the old woman said, then she closed her eyes, smiling and contented that their last moments together were not spent in silence. Stalker carried out his Queen's instructions to the letter, smashing the Black Rat's perimeter, throwing the facility's defenders into disarray and allowing Catherine and Wormsmeat to escape the vile

---

10   Only severe trauma to the skull can destroy a zombie. This durability is another reason zombie workers were in such demand.

institution.

The Harrowers wrought their destruction quickly and soon the greatest Resurrection factory of Cemetery Gate caught fire. As it burned, it made an artificial dawn in the middle of the night. Then the Harrowers, led by Catherine and her faithful zombie, walked out of the Gate and into legend.

BIBLIOGRAPHY.

Kearns-Goodwin, D. (2010) *Henry Clay: Portrait of a President*. Resurgam Press. New York.

Robertson, H. (1987) *Catherine D'Ark: From Rogue to Reformer*. Imperial Press. London.

Scott, B (2005) *Empire of the Dead: How Britain Prospered as a Manufacturer of Zombies*. HUP. Hexford.

Seldhorn, E.(2014) *Damsel Not in Distress – A Life of Evangeline D'Ark*. Magnific Press. Canberra.

Southcott, M. (1997) *The Resurrection Industry from 1650 to the Present*. HUP. Hexford.

Zulbrigge, N. (1982) *Necessary Evil: The Role of Ghoul Gangs in the 19th Century Economy*. Imperial Press. London.

Hungry Again

By Thomas Logan

Rose Wichita Greenfield, Room 213.

The entirety of her hearing is being drowned out by Grace Goodman's, her nemesis and roommate's, blessed flat line noise on her darn monitoring machine. Rose keeps pressing the call button, not that she thinks it'll do any good. People fall, people die. People leave. Like so many of her friends. It's a series of faces that come and go, even the employees, some nicer than others but all in a hurry and all in the end eventually go. Harder and harder to make lasting friends, much less throw bridge parties these days.

Lights outside the aging, two-story retirement home have gone dark. Must have a generator keeping the power on inside, Rose infers. She is reminded how her husband loved looking out the window. He used to spend mornings that way on the weekends sobering up and then on into retirement, just gazing out their front dining room windows. Some days sitting at the table with him she'd see the wood frames of a window as iron bars keeping her in. Others, she thought about her garden. She nearly just about left Art a hundred dozen times. But then what would she do? Once, she made it as far as the bus station. She earned two busted ribs for that. After which, she just worried and waited, waited for Art to die, which he eventually obliged, bequeathing her all his bank loans and gambling debts.

Rose keeps pressing on the switch. Something's not right. Staff should be responding. Her hearing aids are out and she can't see none too well, darker all the time, whether or not she blinks. Her thoughts grow fainter. She keeps pressing the switch.

***

Grace Goodman, Room 213.

The one thing Grace Goodman definitely did not want is to have to go and force it. No, her life's moments should just flash before her eyes all on their own. She should get a chance – she has every right goddammit – to see the good things she's done, all the crap she had put up with, a lifetime in review. *Grace Goodman, this is your life!* Nothing.

So she tries forcing. It's cheating, she knows. Like on the house phone pretending someone's on the other line to make it look like you ain't alone. But Grace is. It's how you enter and leave this world, they say. She's maybe just a bit more alone than most.

Grace herself on the road, travelling with her father.

She couldn't have kids, didn't want to adopt neither. Never been one for charity, second-hand goods, or other people's trash. 'Don't take no pity on me,' Grace said to those who couldn't mind their own goddamn business. She worked her whole goddamn life. And Prince Charming never came. Besides, who knows what she'd get with these spoiled little S.O.B.s these days. Still, be nice if there were someone to take care of her. A son to keep her at his home or some better place where police sirens don't wail away outside.

***

Roger Brown, Room 224.

Roger Brown is a ladies' man. Short women? Sure thing. Tall women? Amen, brother. White women? Mmm, mmm, baby, yes, sir! Some brothers might pretend they don't, maybe had some bad dealings sometime back that sours their milk, but Roger wouldn't kick none of these young White nurse-things out of his bed. In the meantime, until that lucky day comes, he's gotta take matters into his own hand. No man ever went blind jerking it to Wheel of Fortune.

197

When's it on? Oh, that Ms Vanna White.

Not much else to think about when you're made a child again, have to follow the rules of the house, have to hide your bodily doings.

Every time they catch Roger with his manhood in hand, he just gives them a line about – Welp, I guess it here's about time I did the honest thing and settled down and got married – and they get the sarcasm. Some guys get accustomed, thinks Roger, to the waiting to be dead, but I'm gonna be a horn dog till the day I die.

***

Special Agent Sean Finn, First Floor Main Hallway.

Wet on the floor. Can't tell if it's the rain the subjects tracked in or his blood. Shot through the gut, wouldn't you know. He hears the sirens outside. Backup. More meat for the slaughter.

He should have played this differently, not demanded to see the canister in person, arranged the meet in a less populated area. Too late. He respects enterprising NASA scientists less than terrorists and the Klan combined. The virus loose. And his gun arm too weak to put a bullet in his brain.

God help us all.

***

Roger Brown, Room 224.

Just abruptly, sudden jolt of significant noise like spinning around on the radio dial with the speakers on full blast—

He's in and out of consciousness. And sometimes he forgets things. People will just not be there when he's been talking to them, or faces look familiar but he just can't place the name. Names for common things sometimes too. Like cup. Or, uh, …

Roger can hear her hiding under his bed. When did she come in? Nurse with a ripped shirt showing off a naughty red bra.

Young flesh.

"Well, I do say," he begins, hanging over the edge of the bed on his stomach, feeling the rush of blood to his head. "Please," she says and keeps repeating in a whisper. Well, if that ain't an invitation, Robert says to himself.

He's smiling, britches getting tight, when he sees the shadows at the barricaded door. And then recalls the commotion, and then that he is in a world of wrong.

***

Grace Goodman, Room 213.

Applying more honey than naturally occurring vinegar when the special occasion called, Grace had, for more than half her life, tried making them bosses and gentleman friends of hers into husbands. But the older she got, the more disgusting, until she had flesh dangling off her elbows and purple-blue veins out her legs like a river map. Whenever she had insurance, it never covered dental, much less getting rid the birthmark on her face and neck. She tells people she squandered her youth and beauty, but, truth is, she never really was all that young or beautiful. No man ever gave her the time of day for long. When they did, she never got pregnant.

So Grace's been preparing for a lonely death. She'll be dead and cold for a long time, longer than she's been alive.

Like yesterday and the day before and back too many now to count – and so about all she can recall vividly anymore about her life – it's this one same exact goddamn thing, doing what she does now, lying in bed and waiting. Any day now.

Next Saturday-a-week is going to be the last Saturday of the month when she can make pretend with an uncomfortable little Boy Scout boy who will be told to likewise play along. He'll pretend to be her grandson and have to go through her album together with her. Looking at the few old photos of herself alone only makes her more depressed. I look all happy and shit. It's a moment in time she might be remembered by but isn't her. Is gone.

***

Rose Wichita Greenfield, Room 213.

Slower now. She's pushing the button still, the flat line still buzzing in her head. She's been holding her breath. *Lungs*, she tells herself mentally in a whisper, *you can exhale now, pretty please and thank you*. But she can't breathe out.

The generator must be running down. Everything dimmer. This darkness, Rose knows, means she can't read anymore of her Reader's Digests. Why this concerns her so when she can't see a blessed thing, why she is so frightened about magazines going to waste, she can't think to explore.

The last of the old electrical activity is exhausting itself, making way for less troubling, limbic thoughts. It's her own monitor Rose has heard flatline. Her vision now improves courtesy of the compromised canister's chemical agents working their way through the cells of her body. Reading and worrying no longer matter so much. The clicker falls from her hand. Her roommate's health is a distant memory. Replaced by one clear, untroubling desire:

EAT!

***

Grace Goodman, Room 213.

The decrepit are walking again. Grace stumbles out into the hall after dead Rose, keeping her distance. She watches her now former, reanimated roommate stumble down the linoleum toward a group feeding on the floor. Rose Greenfield tries bending gently to sit herself down, but, bad knees, falls.

No teeth, she joins her elderly neighbours' ravenous gnawing, gumming the flesh off the two orderlies' bones. Ghouls with good teeth make the incision, rip a choice piece for themselves before being pushed out the way by greedy mouths and fingers like Rose's.

Grace is repelled. Some swarm logic tells her to seek nourishment elsewhere.

Behind her, a panicked uniformed police officer is being ripped into by a male LRN. He's dressed in pink scrubs with a fist-sized hole in his neck-beard that pieces of swallowed cop flesh fall out from. Miss Goodman hesitates. Some deep neural wiring cautions Grace, warns her that she doesn't belong. The nurse is of a different status, healthy, urban, young. Male. But we're all the same age when we're dead. A new future is birthed before her eyes. Grace Goodman emits a joyful groan and joins her new family feasting in this earthly afterlife.

The Gravedigger

By Liam Hogan

There's a sharp ring of metal against... what? A gravestone? A coffin?

I jerk upright, listening over the moan of the wind. Then I'm out of my cot, reaching for the greatcoat slung across the back of the wicker chair, stooping to lift the army rifle from the bench. It's been a while since I've had to chase grave robbers from these grounds, once it was my reputation as a marksman that stayed them from their sordid task, now... now there are other concerns and the risks far outweigh the meagre rewards.

As I ease the door of the gatehouse open cold air whistles in, ruffling the folds of my unbuttoned coat. From the depths of the dark room behind me a sudden voice commands: "Wait."

I turn and level the rifle at the slim figure that steps into the slanted rectangle of bright moonlight. So, I realise, that I might see him more clearly.

"You must give them longer," he says, ignoring the firearm aimed at his midriff. "It will take them some time."

The ringing is louder now that the door is open; a metallic beat over the familiar anguished howls. "Zombies?" I ask, certain already of the answer.

His lips purse in distaste. "This is 1913, Mr Sanger, not the dark days of primitive superstition. They are not the undead. Never were, and, perhaps, never will be."

I feel my grip tighten on the stock of the Lee-Enfield and ease a finger towards the safety. "What are they doing out there?"

"Merely digging up one of their own. You buried Elizabeth

202

Marshall today, did you not?"

"I did," I reply, defiantly.

"In chains and under concrete?"

"Yes."

"Then as I said, it will take them a while to release her from her binds. They are not, alas, as coordinated as you or I, Mr Sanger."

I stare at him, standing there, once again making free with my name. "And you are?"

He laughs. "Forgive my rudeness. I should have introduced myself. But then, I doubt you would be willing to shake my hand. Perhaps a lowering of that rifle will serve instead?"

I keep the rifle where it is. "You are one of them?"

He tilts his head slightly to one side. "If you like. They – we – are not all simple beasts. It depends on the exact progression of the virus. In some, indeed in most cases, it causes a rapid swelling of the brain, leading to coma and permanent damage to all but the most basic functions: the need to eat, the fear of pain, a desire for the company of their own kind. In others, the effects are less severe; they retain a basic level of intelligence, the ability to understand commands, a distorted and painful memory of what they once were. In rare cases, such as mine, the patient retains all the capacity for thought they ever had and gains much more besides."

"Gains? What gains?"

"Come, Mr Sanger. You have seen enough to know the answer to that. Immortality! Or as close as we are ever likely to get." He takes a step forward, the rifle all but forgotten, daring me to disbelieve him. "Strange, is it not? Something medical experts have sought with such passion down the

203

ages; how vehement their reaction against it, against us! They should be working to cure the unfortunate side-effects, rather than trying to eradicate the disease, rather than trying to destroy the afflicted. I'd hardly call that standing by their sacred oaths, would you?"

"The... afflicted, are classed as legally dead," I observe, neutrally.

"And yet unlike others of your increasingly numerous profession, who separate the head from the neck, burying it at the corpse's feet, or who rush to cremate the comatose, you choose the infinitely more laborious method of internment. Why is that, Mr Sanger?"

Is this why I am still alive? Is this the riddle that stays his hand, that stops him from killing me in my sleep?

"I am a gravedigger," I reply. "It is not my place to pass judgement on those I bury. Merely to ensure that once buried, they stay buried. Hence the chains, hence the concrete. My usual precautions in these troubled times."

He raises an eyebrow. "You do not approve of what my friends are doing out there?"

"No, I do not. Let no-one say I do not do my solemn duty without the due care and diligence it deserves."

"Don't worry," he says, "they will fill in the grave once they are done."

"That," I reply, grimly, "is hardly the point."

"Is it not?" he muses. "Then perhaps we can save each other some effort in future. The people you are burying, they are not dead. If the bodies were not interred with such indecent haste, you would have evidence of that for yourself. But the law dictates that once some ill-informed quack unable or unwilling to detect the frail pulse of someone in a coma signs the notice of decease, then the services of a gravedigger must be employed. Very well. Employ them we shall. But if the coffin were empty?"

"I do not think the Reverend... "

"The Reverend will join our ranks by this time tomorrow," he says. "The bandage he wore on his arm this afternoon covers a nasty bite. One he well deserved, Mr Sanger. He is not as respectful of the dead, or the living, as you are."

I take in this startling news. "May God rest his soul."

The moonlit figure tuts. "You forget. He is not dead, he will not die. And though God has nothing to do with it, I – a mere mortal – may yet influence his fate. Decide if he should retain his faculties, or join those unfortunates he lacked the compassion to pray for and who are incapable of praying for themselves."

"And how would you go about that?" I ask, intrigued. "How do you play at being God?"

He ignores my jibe. "I was a medical man, before. I would be again, given the chance. Prompt action is required. Ice! Cooling the body reduces the swelling of the brain, prevents the injury it causes before the virus puts a stop to apoptosis."

I look at him blankly. "I don't... "

There's a pause, a moment of silence, from both within the gatehouse and without. Then the ringing begins again, erratic, now.

"*Apoptosis* – the Greek for falling away. What your cells are programmed to do, Mr Sanger, when damaged, when attacked. It is not the lack of oxygen, the invasion by a virus, or the cold grip of winter that kills. It is the cells themselves, choosing to die. An imperfect and outdated process, surpassed by modern science and one which this virus arrests.

"If you shoot me you will do physical damage. You will

destroy a small number of cells directly in the path of the bullet. A few thousands, at most. Maybe a million. But why should the death of so few cells lead to the death of the whole? Even if for a while there is no blood reaching my lungs, my brain, why should these organs not spring back to life the moment oxygen rich blood does reach them? That is the blessing of this virus. One no doubt it employs for purely selfish reasons, protecting its host to guarantee its survival, its spread."

"God's will… " I mutter, but again he swiftly interrupts.

"Is tuberculosis God's will? Is cholera? If so then this virus is also his will and it is the duty of all who have the capacity of thought to treat the infected with respect. And yet, the country convulses with fear, with hate! There is little I can do about that, Mr Sanger. The number of us who, like me, can discourse rationally, who might argue our case, is few. So, I ask for your help. And knowing that those you bury are not dead, how can you carry on as before? How can you still claim to be a reputable man?"

I bristle at that, this stranger in the night passing judgement on me, on my profession. If I were to let fly the bullets in my rifle, no court would convict me, to them I would be shooting a dead man.

I think for a moment. His intent is obvious. He aims to hold me here, by talking, while the foul creatures in the graveyard go about their mindless business. He aims to allay my fears by allowing me to train my rifle on him. I wonder if it is even still loaded – how silently he must have crept into my room! If he wanted to dispatch me, he has already had plenty of opportunity.

"You understand," I say, "I cannot be seen to… "

"Do not worry. We will be discreet. And when the time comes-if your time comes – we will move heaven and earth to make sure that you yourself are treated with the utmost care."

I shudder, a reaction that amuses him.

"Come," he says, "lower your weapon. Go back to sleep, if you can. We will be gone well before sunrise and you may consider this night a bad dream. In the morning, when the Reverend falls ill, you will offer to take over the duties of laying him and other unfortunates to rest. You will order in supplies of ice, money will be provided. And you will leave me a set of keys to the Chapel of Rest."

He takes a step forward, his eyes trained on me, and another step, until the barrel of the rifle is a hand's width from his waistcoat. I lower the weapon, though I keep my hands firmly on it. "What will you – and your companions – do?" I ask. "You will never be accepted here."

"Even when we outnumber the uninfected?" He smiles. "But you are right. We will leave these lands. There is a turmoil in Europe, the death throes of imperialistic empires. There will be war, Mr Sanger. A war unlike any seen before. A war that cries out for a race of men less prone to injury, less fearful of death. Our war. We will prove our worth on the battlefields."

I look on him in renewed horror. I saw action in the second Boer War, learnt my trade there, and though this Doctor claims to be a rational man, I find his posturing more frightening than even the thought of his lumbering friends out in the graveyard.

"Do you really think you are so indestructible?" I ask. "Have you no weaknesses at all?"

A cloud darkens his countenance, whether cast by my scornful tone, or I perhaps I had chanced upon a sore spot, I could not tell.

"Medicine will catch up. There is already a cure for syphilis and more will surely follow. Science will conquer all of the ills, Mr Sanger, even influenza! Even perhaps, the virus that gifts us immortality. But then, why would we want

207

to do that?"

There's a peal of staccato thunder as five metal shells drop to the floor around his feet, and my finger convulses on the trigger of the empty rifle. When I look up again he is at the door, staring at me with those eyes – those very distinctive eyes.

"Now, if you'll excuse me, I need to attend to poor Lizzie. The woman you buried alive today is my sister. Did I mention that?"

He steps backwards into the night.

"I do hope she's not in too bad a state, Mr Sanger. I really do. For your sake."

The Call of the Loons

By Jared Wright

Night forced its way upon them again. No lights showed in the cabin. The father's silhouette blanketed most of the bay window. The barrel of the shotgun glistened in the moonlight. A floor board creaked under the boy's weight.

"What are you doing, sneaking around in here?" the father asked.

"I can't sleep."

"And why not?"

"The loons."

The call of the loons on the lake went out like manic giggles from those long drowned.

"They do seem loud tonight," the father said. He scratched his chin and smiled at the boy. "Them birds ain't going to hurt you."

"Will you stay by the bed?" the boy asked.

The father thought for a moment, allowing the loon cries to penetrate the walls.

"I guess it's 'bout time I took a rest."

The night enveloped them as they lay in their sleeping bags. Both fell asleep with time, but the loons carried on.

***

In the morning, the boy awoke to find the father on the front porch. The gun laid across his lap, an open can of beans in his hand. He offered the food to the boy.

"Can we go fishing?" the boy asked. He took the can and

tasted the processed barbeque flavor.

"Can't even leave the porch. I saw one of them down there again."

When they originally arrived at the cabin, the father told him of the bears, their taste for human flesh, and curiosity for lights at night. The boy never witnessed any bears. "I wish they were dead."

"Why would you say a thing like that?" the father asked.

"I'm sick of the cabin. I want to go home. I miss my mom and dad."

"We can't leave," the father said, pulling at his white collar. "The bears would eat us."

"Why have I not seen a bear?"

"They come before you wake up."

"I want to see one."

"Maybe we should go back inside."

***

The loons continued their nightly racket as the boy lay on his back, staring up into the darkness. The father snored next to him. The boy tossed around the idea of going back to sleep, but a greater urge began to eat away at him. He slipped out of the sleeping bag and went to the door, cautious of stepping over the creaky floorboard.

His face pressed against the glass of the window, looking toward the lake. The water visibly shimmered in the moonlight. The call of the loons came ashore. The boy put on his boots and unlocked the door. The latch echoed through the cabin, and he froze, afraid the father would sit up and grab the shotgun – nothing happened. The boy stepped into the cool air. He stopped at the edge of the porch, listening to the sounds of the forest.

Loons cried out, bugs hummed, and branches cracked as animals moved their way through the night. No bears growled, but he walked with caution. The dew soaked his bare legs as he moved through the tall grass. The loon noises grew deafening as he reached the shore. He could see the birds, floating on top of the water – small blemishes on the surface. Picking the largest rock his strength would allow, the boy threw it into the water. The bird calls grew louder for a second – then dissipated into silence.

He laughed. They returned his call, drawing near to his location. Branches to his left began to break. Like the loons, the branches began to snap closer to where he stood. He remembered the father's advice of swimming into the lake if a bear came close. Bears could not swim – according to the father – so the diving pallet in the middle of the lake promised a safe haven.

The bushes to his left began to shuffle as the loons drew closer behind him. The boy took off his boots, preparing his body for the swim ahead. Grunts and moans erupted from the brush. Suddenly, the greenery parted, allowing – not a bear – a man to step through. The boy sighed with relief, waving.

"Can you help me?" the boy asked. "I've been kidnapped by a priest. My parents live... "

His mouth hung open as the man staggered forth. His clothes, ripped and tattered, clung to his body, weighed down by dark splotches which gleamed in the dim light. He came at the boy, letting out a growl, almost bear-like. The boy opened his mouth to scream. Before he could, the man's head exploded. Brain matter splattered across the sand. The father stood a few feet away, partially hidden by the pines.

"What are you doing out here?" he asked.

"I came out to look at the loons."

"We need to get back inside."

"What was that man?" the boy asked.

"Get inside, then I'll tell you."

"Is that why we had to leave mom and dad?"

Before the father could answer, the forest erupted into a stereo of gurgled moans. Others, just like the man, stumbled out into the open. First there came ten, then fifty, then even more.

"They found us," the father said. He turned to the boy. "Swim to the pallet. Go."

The crazed look in the eyes of the others froze the boy in his place.

"Damn it, boy. Don't tell me I did this all for nothing. Swim."

The father turned away from him and began to shoot. The grotesque fireworks display sprayed the woods with gore. The boy dove into the water and swam through its cool veils, just as his dad taught him years ago. The loons called out ahead of him, as if leading the way. After he surfaced on the pallet the gun shots ceased. The boy thought he would never be warm or safe again. He looked to the shore and saw the horde of others piling onto one spot, like football players tackling the ball carrier – and eating him.

The lapping of the waves against the boards did little to calm his nerves. The others began to remove themselves from the pile and stumbled around. They never went near the water. Within twenty minutes the whole scene cleared, leaving a peaceful lake shore.

***

The boy awoke the next day, blinking away the sunrise. He could not remember falling asleep and recalled only the carnage from the night before. The shore appeared clear. Everything looked fine, as if nothing happened. He thought it could have been a dream, for the only thing to fear in the woods – realistically – were bears.

The splash disrupted a school of sunfish as he jumped into the water. The icy chill shocked his body into momentary paralysis. He used the pallet to propel himself. As he drew closer, he saw the ominous red stains in the sand and knew no dream ever occurred, only a living nightmare. He walked the short distance to the bundle, fighting the shivers which barred his body from doing anything. The frayed remains of the father's shirt left nothing to the imagination. A few bones lay scattered. The white collar stained red. Small pieces of rubbery flesh strewn about. The boy wanted to scream. He wanted to vomit. But he felt safe as if the frigid chill of the lake refused to allow emotion into his mind and body.

The boy looked around but saw no sign of the others. A loon called out in the early hours. Its echo hovered all around the mountains which surrounded the lake. The boy began to move towards the cabin – alone – unaware of the open door and the shelter the others had taken.

Life Lessons

Bygones

By Pete Aldin

Daron awoke to find his face pressed sideways on his desk blotter, one cheek slippery with drool. He sat bolt upright in his chair, wiped at his face. A dislodged quill dropped nib-down onto the desk and stuck fast in the wet patch. Noise – it was the noise that had awoken him. The commotion in the park opposite his rooms meant that the Festival of Souls was already in full swing.

"Of all the days to be caught napping!" He pushed himself off the chair and stumbled away from his desk toward the front window, still mumbling. "You're getting sloppy, Daron. Sloppy will get you dead."

Or penniless, he thought. *Which is just as bad.*

He allowed himself one long peek through the crack in the curtains before drawing them tightly closed. He passed a frilled cuff over his clammy forehead. Ferris wasn't coming for him. At least, not yet.

Will he even come this year? he wondered. *His brother can't have enough money to get him raised again, surely.*

He sagged against the window frame, listened to the clatter of horses and the rumble of carriages in the streets around the park, necrogeners from all over town ferrying in the freshly resurrected to rendezvous with those paying for their resurrections. Somewhere nearby, a flute tootled a happy tune, and a fiddle followed along – badly. But that was to be expected: dead musicians often lost their ear.

The Festival of Souls, Daron thought sourly. The living and the dead pretending for a day that death is not the end, that love can endure forever, that bygones need not remain bygones.

Normally Daron didn't object to festivals. Festivals were

good for business, after all, especially *his* business. People needed loans in the days leading up to them to buy extra food and wine for guests, to bribe their gods with offerings, to have their loved ones raised from the dead.

But Ferris's surprise-visit last year had certainly taken the shine from this particular celebration. If Ferris was going to make a longstanding habit of it, then the Festival of Souls had become more trouble than it was worth. For Daron, at least.

A pox on Ferris! he thought, rubbing at tired eyes, then realized it was a futile wish. *A pox upon his brother then!*

Perhaps if he wasn't actually in his office, Ferris would give it up. After all, no one came looking for loans *on* Festival days, so there was no business to be lost. Perhaps there was still time to leave, jump in a coach, flee town and return tomorrow.

As long as Ferris wasn't out there already.

He parted the curtain sharply and dust ballooned out around him. His maid had obviously decided to get herself in the Festival mood by winding down her cleaning over the past few days. Lazy wench. He'd make her work doubly hard on the morrow, hangover or no hangover.

His eyes scoured the park outside his office and the street between. Each year at this time, the view was the same. The newly resurrected slowly regaining their wits. Old women holding hands with their departed husbands, staring lovingly into their eye sockets. Worshippers of Systatos the Cadaver God dancing with the dead, singing hymns, and interrupting picnickers to invite them to join their Church. Parents playing marbles in the sunshine with departed children, children eternally five or six or nine years old, children who would vanish again at sunset...

"And then there's Ferris," Daron muttered, catching a glimpse of the dead man staggering right through a ring of dancing Systites, ignoring their requests to join in. He let the curtain fall back in place. "Bloody Ferris. Coming for me again."

He backed up to the opposite wall, praying to gods he normally ignored. His hand dropped to the lever concealed in the wall, tucked inside a lantern sconce. He'd use it if necessary, open the trapdoor when Ferris burst into the room. Just like last year. Watch Ferris plunge into the cage in the cellar. Just like last year. And put up with a day of impotent moaning and cage-rattling as Ferris tried to get out while Daron got on with his bookwork.

Just like last year.

It had worked once. It would probably work again.

The dead have such terrible memories.

But although the body would be gone at sunset – dissipated back to the underworld by whatever spell the Necrogeners used – the whole thing was still a damned inconvenience.

Something struck the door – the dull thump of flesh on wood. Daron jumped. Outside, Ferris moaned. The door handle rattled. Daron was glad he'd remembered to lock it this year. Last year, he hadn't been expecting this kind of company.

Perhaps if I'm quiet, he'll give up. Perhaps he'll think I left town for the day.

The door shuddered as something else crashed into it. A crack appeared in the wood. *Curse it! He has an axe this year. His brother must have thought of that.* Another blow and another. Chips of wood flew into the room and daylight spewed through the hole. His hands trembled on the lever.

A pause and then another harder blow widened the hole in the door. *I'll have to buy another door, damn it. More expense.* Ferris's pale angry face became visible for a moment, peering

218

in. Daron felt himself flinch and he wished he'd thought to buy an axe of his own, something to defend himself if for some reason the trapdoor failed to open. He winced at the thought. *When* was *the last time I oiled the release catch?*

Seeing Daron, the dead man leered and resumed chopping.

Why didn't I kill both *of them when I had the chance?*

Ferris and Londo, brothers, moneylenders, formerly known as The Competition.

Undoubtedly Londo was the one raising Ferris each year in this attempted retribution. Londo, who'd always been shy of violence and intimidation, preferring to build a business by offering 'good service,' whatever that was. Londo, who had talked his brother out of letting Daron buy them out. Londo, who had stupidly tried to resist the group of men armed with axe-handles whom Daron sent to chase The Competition out of town... and had gotten his brother killed in the ensuing mêlée.

"It's your own stupid fault!" he called out. "Should have taken the money when you both had the chance!"

The axe bit deep and in pulling it out, Ferris tore a chunk of wood the size of Daron's head from the door. He moaned with the effort.

Daron's fingers closed tighter around the lever. He forced himself to remain calm.

I'll win this. It's a simple matter of timing, of waiting till he steps inside and onto the trapdoor. And then tomorrow, I'll send Mung and Hakkit out to take care of Londo, so this never happens again.

Londo.

Where Londo had gone to live after being run out of town – and *how* he'd afforded the Necrogeners' fees to bring his

219

brother back – Daron didn't know. Perhaps Londo had taken to a life of banditry, waylaying travellers in and out of the city. If that was so, then he was due a little more respect than Daron had formerly given him. He was learning.

You get what you take from this world. No more, no less.

He forced a laugh. "What you take from this world." There was a reanimated man bashing down his door who wanted to take *Daron* out of the world.

"Well, you *won't* take me, Ferris!" he called. "Go find something else to do with your one day of life! Have a drink! Dance with a Systite!"

The axe made a *clunk* as it hit the front step, chipping the stonework. *More bloody repair work.* The dead man forced his already ragged body through the break in the door, tearing the clothes he'd been buried in. He stood swaying with one hand clutching the broken door behind him for balance. His sunken eyes glared with the kind of malevolence only a corpse could muster.

Daron steeled himself. The trap door – he'd had it installed years ago for incursions like this – lay a short step inside the room. If he pulled the lever too early, Ferris might dart back and avoid the trap. Too late, and the dead man might be upon him.

He cursed the laws governing festivals. *Where are Mung and Hakkit when I need them? Holidays shouldn't apply to men-at-arms. Who's to protect their masters?*

Ferris growled and Daron found himself snarling back. "Come on then, lad. Might as well get it over with. Come and give me a big hug."

Ferris rushed forward and Daron pulled the lever.

***

Daron stood in the doorway of the cellar and watched

Ferris raging against the bars of his cage. Some of the dead man's skin had already rubbed raw across his fingertips and palms where he'd scraped at the iron joins and clasps.

"That's solid iron, idiot," Daron said. "Just sit still and wait it out. Maybe think about giving up this silly game. How about at next year's Festival you and your brother take the day off, rest up, go fishing?"

Next year.

What if Mung and Hakkit couldn't find Londo before then? He wondered if it was possible to be rid of Ferris some other way.

Perhaps he could lead him away from the office to somewhere he could set him on fire, burn the pesky fellow to a crisp. No, that would do no good. Nor would chopping him into a thousand pieces and feeding him to the town piggery. The Necrogeners would still bring him back the following year, as long as someone paid them to.

No, the answer is finding Londo and taking care of him.

It took Daron a moment to realize that the annoying corpse had stopped struggling to get out of the cage. And a little longer to realize that Ferris's sunken eyes were not actually staring at him but at a point behind him. He was about to turn when he heard the creak on the stair that announced it was all over.

His head snapped forward as something hit him, hard. The world went black just before he hit the ground.

***

When Daron woke, the world was upside down. And moving from side to side.

"What—?" he asked, his voice catching in his throat. "What's—?"

221

He bent his neck to look down. No, not down – *up!* His feet and ankles were tied to a joist in the cellar ceiling.

Dangling like a side of pork. How did it come to this?

"Look, Ferris," a voice said. "Our friend is awake."

Daron stiffened. *Londo!*

Ferris moaned, and Londo responded. "What's that, brother? You want to hurt Daron? Sure you can. This is your special day. With twelve hours left until sunset, we can do plenty of hurting."

Ferris made a happy sound.

Londo's lean face and bug-eyes moved into Daron's field of vision. His hair was greyer than Daron remembered, his face more lined. A couple of years of poverty had not treated Londo kindly, and Daron almost felt sorry for him. Almost.

"'Allo, Daron. Miss us?"

"Londo! It's nice to see you again. Why don't you cut me down from here, and we'll talk about, uh, financial compensation. Business. Eh?"

Londo turned his head to look at Ferris, lurking somewhere behind Daron. "Did you get that? No, I don't understand what he's saying, either. Never mind. It's time to send *him* a message."

Daron flinched as Londo slipped a filleting knife from a sheath on his belt.

"Don't ya just love the Festival of Souls, Ferris?" Londo said, running a finger along the back of the blade. "Same old thing every year, but it never loses its shine."

Daron felt his brow twist in a frown. What was the scoundrel talking about?

"Yep," said Londo. "I might be getting old, but this *never* does."

"What do you mean?"

"You sound confused there, Daron." Londo leaned in and grabbed Daron's shirtfront, carefully slitting the cloth. Daron tried to wriggle free, but Londo's grip was too strong. Ferris lurched into view now, excitement visible on his misshapen face. "Oh, you don't remember it. Neither does he," he added, pointing the blade at Ferris. "But we did this last year. And the year before. And the year before that too. I think this is the twelfth time. But I never was good at numbers. That was more Ferris's department than mine. Tell you what I have become good at, though."

Londo lifted and twisted the blade right in front of Daron's left eye.

Daron pulled his face away from it, neck straining. "What do you mean *last year?* Last year, he came for me. Ferris came for me, not you. And I... I... "

How had it ended? Daron suddenly realized he couldn't remember. And that terrified him, almost as much as the slim slick blade that danced before his eyes.

"Ah, I think I understand what you're saying now." He pointed to Daron's mouth. "The voice takes a while to get used to. Hell, it's taken me *years.*" He laughed. "Yes, Ferris came for you last year. And you put him in the cage. And I hit you over the head. And I let Ferris out. And we went ahead and did what we're about to do now."

Daron stared. *No! NO!! That's not possible!*

"The dead have such terrible memories." Londo heaved a melodramatic sigh. "Every damn year you forget, Daron. And I think that's what makes this so much fun." Londo stepped back and smiled at his brother. "You go first this year, Ferris. I think it's your turn. And you sure earned it."

Ferris leant in, ignoring the proffered knife. A moment later Daron felt scabby nails close around his scrotum. Through the noise of his own scream, Daron heard Londo say, "I just love the Festival of Souls. Best damn day of the year."

Leftovers

By Sean Kavanagh

She'd never heard of the town of Erith and hoped she'd soon forget it existed. Far enough from London to fall off the radar of even the most creative real estate agent, but still somehow urban and grey.

The official car that she had managed to beg got lost three times on its way to the press conference. The driver, a cheerful Cockney Bangladeshi swearing at his satnav in a variety of languages as it took him down dead end after dead end. Which is all there were in this part of Southern England.

Jessica Toombs was the junior minister for 'Special Welfare Measures,' which was the equivalent of being sent to the Northern Ireland Office in the 1970s. She was never quite sure who she had made an enemy of to land the job. Maybe her face didn't fit. Or more likely her uterus didn't fit. As soon as this new wave of 'Supplementary Foodbanks' had been announced, she knew that her chinless chickenshit boss would want to put a country mile between him and the project. To be fair, it hadn't been his idea, but as flat as Whitehall was, shit still rolled downhill. From Prime Minister, to Minister to… her. She wasn't in the old boys club, so she lived permanently at the bottom of shit hill.

"Here!" announced the driver with some relief. Usually foodbanks were cynically located in churches or school basements – places associated with charity and social progress – but this one had been dumped down by uncaring hands in that bit of land between London and the coast. One of the planners described its location as being like 'that bit of skin between your arsehole and your balls.' Jessica had pointed out to him she didn't have balls, but the guy's description has been unfortunately accurate.

She looked down at her notes. Her speech. The minister

225

had given her key phrases and buzzwords he insisted she repeat again and again: simplify the message until even the dumbest man could understand it (years later she found out that was something Hitler had said). Foodbanks – the ultimate admission of failure in western civilisation. Just enough to stop people starving, but toxic enough politically that even the opposition parties ignored their existence. They stank of everyone's failure. People being handed out cans of soup and chocolate bars to survive and all less than fifty miles from the City of London where billionaires roamed the unregulated savannahs of the global markets.

And they were expanding, covering the land with their failure. A modern blight.

The government's new watchword was *Everyone Should Eat.* A nice easy soundbite for an election year.

"Want me to wait?" asked her driver looking around nervously.

"Of course I bloody do, it's seven miles to the nearest bus stop!"

"Yer, I'll probably wait then," replied the driver losing himself in the sporting pages of his newspaper. Jessica noted the 'probably,' but decided not to argue. At least the press were all inside – no running one of those ambush gauntlets she'd seen all too often on TV.

***

The 'New Prospect' foodbank was sited inside exactly the sort of building that nobody wanted anymore: a three story block of the brutal, jagged concrete that even the trendiest urban hipsters would have trouble getting excited over on their Instagram feeds. Tiny windows two metres from the floor stopped people from looking in or looking out. A hidden place. A place where shameful transactions could happen.

Jessica pushed open the heavy door and stuck her head

226

in. The place looked deserted. A long hallway with doors off it. The sort of thing hallways tend to look like.

"Hello!" she shouted out into the emptiness.

"Hello to you," came an unexpectedly cheery reply. It was followed by the man who who'd called the reply out. Thin, cheap suit, 1990s looking spectacles. He looked every inch the local council official he was. Jessica groaned inside.

"Delighted to meet you," she said, shaking the thin man's hand. She pretended to look delighted, but wasn't really sure what the end result on her face was.

"Can I get you some oxtail soup?" asked the man.

"Sorry?"

The man sniggered to himself. "Sorry, it's all the vending machine does now."

"I'm a vegetarian," she lied. "But thank you. This way, is it?" Jess pointed down the corridor to the lit room at the end.

As they started walking, the cheerfulness of the council man evaporated. He looked nervous. "I'm not used to big events," he confessed.

"Big?" asked Jess, concerned. They'd tried to keep it low-key back at the ministry, but it only took one drunken intern with Twitter to screw up these things.

"Yes, twenty reporters, maybe more. Some of them are even real ones from newspapers and the telly."

"The telly eh? They must be real then," Jess swore under her breath. This wasn't the work of a drunken kid, she'd been nicely set up by her boss. She was going to be the face of 'Foodbank Britain' after this. *Everyone Should Eat...*

They stopped at the door.

Then, it was a scene all too familiar. The scrum of reporters, cameras, smart phones, and one older hack with an actual tape recorder. A micro camera drone buzzed her, turned came back and accidentally collided with her head.

"Ouch!" She swatted at it like a fly.

"Sorry," yelled the operator.

"Please, no camera drones!" barked the little council man. "And if everyone could take a step or two back from the podium we can start the questions."

Jessica shot the man a look. Questions?! There wasn't meant to be a Q&A. This was a roll out, a short speech, press the button or whatever and then a few photos.

"Miss Toombs!" called one reporter.

"No, questions later please," continued the council man, locking them into his earlier mistake. Now she was screwed, she thought.

With a heavy sense of loss – job loss most likely – Jessica Toombs, the junior minister for 'Special Welfare Measures' walked behind the podium. The room went quiet. So quiet it didn't seem normal.

"Thank you all for coming today." She cringed inside at her prepared text. A turd on paper, it sounded even more turd-worthy on her lips. "As you know, our innovative new 'Everyone Should Eat' programme is aimed at extending the basic right of food provision to all in our society. Whether newcomers or people who have lived here all their lives, no matter what lifestyle, people are knitted together by our common need for food. If—"

"Are you ashamed?" heckled a tabloid reporter she vaguely recognised.

"Please questions at the end!" The council man shot back.

"No, no," Jessica replied, "let him ask." *The sooner this is over...*

"It's a simple question: Are you ashamed? Is anyone in Whitehall or the government ashamed?"

She looked at him for a few seconds, trying to conjure up emotion that really wasn't there. "If there were hungry mouths, I would indeed be ashamed, but no, this has been measured up and in the real world, this programme *is* the best solution to food provision shortfall."

The reporter snorted. "Nicely done. Maybe a tear next time too eh? Really sell it to us."

"Foodbanks stop hunger!" she barked back with enough force to suggest she was still acting. Which she was.

Everyone Should Eat...

"Go on then, look them in the eye." The reporter pointed over to a group of people standing just to the side. God, how long had *they* been there, Jessica thought. She looked at the underprivileged rabble and felt no pity for the ten men and women. She'd grown up on a council estate, probably with less than most of them, and look at her now.

The tabloid journalist was on his feet.

"Want me to read you their names? The people who come through these doors have names," he taunted her.

"I know their names: Mark Caddell, Janet Caddell, Thomas Negash, Jade O'Malley... shall I go on?" Jessica felt herself swelling. Maybe it was the worst assignment, the worse day of her career, but at least she'd done her homework.

"All right, you made your point. But this is about food, not a pub quiz. Our polls show that people are split deeply on this." Unexpectedly the tabloid man sat down. He'd shot his bolt, and now he wasn't going to be able to read out the names of ten people, he had no plan B. Jessica loved little victories, she thought to herself. Almost more than big wins.

"Please, look at the men and women here today at this foodbank, go on, look." The crowd made a bit of a show of looking. Snapped a few extra pictures. Jessica looked too and hated what she saw: fat, lazy people with a dull bovine stare from the stupidity of their little lives. Drugs probably too. Most of them had glazed over eyes. God she hated them. "Why do people end up in places like this? Bad luck, good luck, waiting in a line? People end up here because they fail to turn up for benefit appointments. People end up here because they spend their money on junk food, instead of the cheap nutritious foods they could buy. Lottery tickets and cheap booze. And drugs. You don't 'end up here,' you make your life choices and they lead you here." She let her words hang. The man from the Daily Mail was nodding like a cheap fairground prize. There was a buzz, a change in their body language. Jessica knew she'd won most of them over.

Everyone Should Eat...

Then, out of the blue (and even some of the red), people started to applaud. Even Jessica was taken aback. People's hatred of the poor was always a useful get-out, but this was amazing. How her boss was going to be pissed off. She wasn't even sure herself how she'd turned this toxic mess around.

"Please," she said gesturing modestly, "please, let's not forget this about the opening of this first, new and unique foodbank. I believe there is a button?" Jessica looked at the council man, who smiled and walked over with a silver box with a big red button on it. The button said 'FOOD'. Jessica waved the remote controlled-button at the press so they could get their photos. She allowed a hint, an echo of smile to escape her lips. No time to blow it now, she thought. Don't overdo it.

"I declare this foodbank, open!"

She pressed the button. Everyone looked over at the ten

people standing to the side. Their blank faces registered nothing. A big mechanical door opened with a hiss. Motors climbed up to speed and then the ten people were moving along on the conveyor belt they were standing on. One by one they disappeared beyond the heavy metal door. The last one in, the door sealed automatically.

Jessica looked down at her shoes.

The first screams came from the chamber. Then the pity-filled bangs against the door. Inside the zombies feasted on the ten poor, poor people.

Everyone Should Eat...

In the Absence of Dignity

By Lee Glenwright

I don't know if I can do it. God help me, I don't know if I can. The gun, as small and as light as it is, feels so heavy in my hands.

I promised that I'd do it if and when the time was right. I swore that I would. And believe me, I had every intention of doing so. But so very many promises are made in the heat of the moment, only to be remembered with regret when the day to honour them finally dawns.

I'm so sorry. I really am.

There are cornerstones. World events that shape and define whole generations, that manage to embed themselves in your mind, in the minds of everyone, a sort of group consciousness. The Americans say that everyone remembers where they were on the day JFK was assassinated. Then it was, *where were you on 9/11? Or 7/7?*

For the record, I do remember where I was the day Kennedy died, I'd just gotten my first proper job, working as a junior in an accounting firm. I'd left school about two years earlier, known Catherine for about a year and a half of that. We were both so young – and she was so beautiful, even then.

Back in those days it all seemed to mean so much more. People waited until the time was right. *We* waited, it was the done thing. Waiting, always waiting. It was another three years almost before I finally ended her waiting and asked her to marry me. She accepted, tears glistening in those huge blue eyes of hers.

"Why are you crying?" I asked. I'll admit, I've never been the most perceptive of men.

"Because it feels like I've waited so long," came her reply, choking back laughter through the tears. "These aren't tears of sadness, George, they're tears of joy. Our joy."

We were married a little over six months later. I promised her then that I'd never hesitate again. Alongside all the stuff about love and honour, I've always tried to hold myself to that promise, I really have.

I just haven't always found it that easy.

September the eleventh, two thousand and one, two days after my fifty-eighth birthday, three years before I was to use the settlement from my early retirement to buy that isolated house in the country that we'd both seen as our dream home for so long. Like millions of other people, I remember watching the footage play over and over again on the television, like an old video cassette stuck on a loop. It's true what they all said, somehow the whole world couldn't quite believe it. It was so much like some awful dream. A little piece of innocence was lost forever on that day, blown to pieces over sacrosanct American airspace, never to return. The whole world changed, that's what everyone said. And it was true, in a sense.

Cathy and I held each other just that little closer from that day onward.

Just in case.

Moments in time that all seem so significant, but mean so little now, when you take a step back from everything and look at the bigger picture.

I wonder just how many people will be left in the days, weeks and months still to come, to say that they remember where they were when the world ended.

It was a day just like so many others, in so many ways. Life was pretty straightforward since my retirement. Some people would call it dull, but as far as I've always been concerned, 'dull' needn't always be such a bad thing. I prefer the term 'simple.' That sounds much nicer.

It was a Spring afternoon, surprisingly warm for the time of year. Cathy was in the garden, tending to her pet rose bushes – excuse me – private joke. I'd always said that we didn't need any children or animals in the house, just as long as she had her garden to look after. I've never been particularly green-fingered myself, so I was in the kitchen, preparing the evening meal. Trying to tempt her away from her roses and her *lavaterae* with the smell of beef stew, complete with freshly baked rustic bread, carrying out onto the gentle afternoon breeze. I'm no chef, not by any stretch of the imagination, but I can follow a recipe when called upon to do so.

"George? What's that awful noise?" Cathy's voice drifted in from the direction of the garden. I was so wrapped up in what I was doing, I hadn't noticed the radio acting up.

"Sorry sweetheart," I called back. "I'll sort it out. Just the radio on the blink again." I've always been one of those people who hates silence, finding that the absence of noise usually gives the mind too good a chance to conjure up its own. At the same time I've always been a bit of an AM/FM man, never had the time for those digital things, you know, the ones that make some annoying pig-like squeal whenever they lose their signal. I'd been so wrapped up in what I was doing that I hadn't even noticed the music had been replaced by the empty static drone of white noise. I fiddled with the aerial a bit and, when that produced no result, gently tapped the radio on one side, the taps slowly growing into impatient thumps with my fist. Stupid bloody thing. With a last stubborn hiss, the crackling of nothingness was replaced once again by the sound of a somewhat serious sounding voice,

-ing back on the air now, after that slight technical problem. Apologies again... looks like we've got it fixed now...

"Sorry love," I called out again. "Sounds like there was a problem with the broadcast. They say it's been sorted out now, though."

"That's okay," she said, still rooting around on her knees. "Almost done here." She stood up and wiped her hands down the front of her special gardening smock. She came across to the window and lifted the brim of her deliberately oversized rattan hat, sunlight glinting off those large blue eyes of hers as she did so.

"Hmmm, that smells good love, when'll it be ready?"

It seemed like nothing at the time, so ordinary, so nondescript. With hindsight, I suppose you could say that was day one.

***

"Have you seen this?" I asked Cathy over breakfast the next morning. "Sounds like it's all over the news."

"What's that dear?" she asked, dabbing away at her mouth with a tissue as she spoke.

I shook out the morning newspaper, sending a spray of toast crumbs scattering across the table as I held it up for her to see. "Sorry... look at this though."

SPACE PROBE WIPEOUT

Then under that,

RETURNING SATELLITE CAUSES COMMUNICATION CHAOS

"So what does that mean?" She asked in that tone of voice that really meant, 'I'm not really interested, but I'll humour you.'

"Not sure. Some science gibberish or other. Boffins at NASA sent up a probe to investigate a solar flare. Then it goes on to use words like 'telemetry' and 'radiation malfunction.' Doesn't really mean that much to me."

"Me neither," she admitted, still sounding as though she'd rather I spoke about something she actually had some interest in.

"Sounds to me like the Americans sent something up into space, probably costing a few billion dollars no doubt, and it's come crashing back down in more than one piece. Probably what sent the radio up the spout yesterday. Had the same effect everywhere, according to this." I took a sip of tea and leaned back, satisfied that I'd made my point.

"Why is it always the Americans starting it?" she asked, putting her own cup down. "They've always got to go that little step further."

"Typical," I said. "Anyway, it'll be all over the news for a few days, no doubt, then it'll all be forgotten about." She nodded in silent agreement, chewing on another mouthful of toast.

How wrong we both were.

That was day two.

***

I suppose the third day was when it all really kicked in, although even then, it didn't feel real somehow. Not at first, more like a bad dream. Breakfast time – I flicked the radio on, as was my habit, expecting to hear some morning smooth jazz. I've always thought that you can't beat a bit of easy listening to set you up for the day.

What came instead was a further announcement, sounding even more serious than the day before. I probably would've laughed out loud at just how gravely it came across, but for the subject matter:

- That news once again. Receiving reports from multiple sources, that bodies of the recently deceased have shown signs of so-called 're-animation.'

"What?"

I almost spat out my mouthful of coffee, pebble-dashing the table in the process. It went on,

Eyewitness reports from morgues and funeral homes suggest that recently deceased bodies are returning to life. Furthermore, it seems reports are beginning to filter through to the effect that, those bodies that are returning are attacking the living.

"Cathy, love," I shouted. "Can you hear this?"

"Hear what, sweetheart?" she called back from the front room, where she was probably straightening the cushions or some other such meaningless job.

"What's the date today?"

"The Ninth of May, why?" Her voice became clearer and I turned to see that she'd abandoned her cushion plumping to join me, presumably drawn by curiosity.

"Definitely *not* April Fool's day, then?"

"No dear, why, what is it?" She seemed oblivious to the sarcasm in my voice, either that or she's simply become used to it over the years.

"There's a man on the radio, says dead bodies are coming back to life and attacking people." The look of disbelief I thought to be on my face must have convinced her that I wasn't making it up. Not that I've ever been one for practical jokes.

"It must be some sort of a prank, surely." Her face now had an expression pretty similar to how I imagined mine to be.

"No, listen," I insisted. "He sounds really serious about it." She pulled out a chair – it scraped noisily against the floor, tiles threatening to drown out the sound of the radio as she did so, and sat alongside me.

- That news again. Reports filtering across from multiple locations worldwide now suggest that the bodies of the dead are returning to life and, in some cases attacking human vic—

I switched the radio off.

"George?" she asked, her voice trembling. Cathy was always that bit more easily led than I like to tell myself I was.

"Rubbish. Absolute rubbish. It *must* be," I insisted, shaking my head in disbelief. "It just isn't possible. Dead bodies can't come back to life!"

I walked through to the lounge and flicked on the television. When we were younger, we used to have a saying, that people wouldn't believe anything unless they'd seen it on television. After a few seconds, the screen lit up. I was expecting to see some newsreader – some *serious* newsreader – exposing the radio hoax,

...As you can see, scenes of panic, estimated to be on a near-global scale, as reanimated corpses begin to attack the—

This time, for good measure, the sombre tones were accompanied by various images of violence, much of it presented in all its bloody, grainy, self-shot, camera phone glory.

I felt my face drain of colour. Trembling now, I turned to look at Cathy, afraid of what I might see. I'd told her it wasn't – *couldn't be –* true and, here I was, exposed as a liar. A powerless liar whose world had suddenly been turned upside down. After all, we belonged to a generation that had been brought up to believe that television *never* lies.

"George?" she said, shaking just as much as I was, trying to hold back tears. "What's happening?"

I turned back to the television just in time to see the news footage. A figure could be made out, lurching along, just like

238

any drunk. His arms were outstretched, as though struggling to maintain his balance and his clothing appeared dirty and dishevelled. He appeared to make a sudden lunge toward the person holding the camera when suddenly, a gunshot rang out and the top of his head sheared away in a bloody spray. His body toppled backward, landing in a crude sprawl on the road. I flinched at the sight, before switching the set off once again.

"What's happening?" That same question again, sniffling as she tried to keep the tears at bay.

I didn't have an answer.

***

Voices. Saying everything and answering nothing.

- *Politicians around the world moving to stem the tide of what has rapidly escalated into hysteria of near pandemic proportions...*

- *Military forces are mobilised as martial law is expected to take effect in most countries...*

So many voices, all saying so many things and saying them all at the same time.

- *Sources have been speculating that reanimated corpses can be stopped only by damage to the head or the brain...*

- *Damage to the brain, or severance of the brain from the rest of the body will incapacitate the walking dead...*

So confusing. So much not making sense.

- *Emergency refuges, now under military jurisdiction...*

- *Aim for the head...*

- *Switchover to BBC Emergency long wave broadcast...*

Confusion. Panic. Fear. Terror.

- Aim for the head. Just aim for the head...

- Emergency refuges... overrun... too many... overwhelming...

Helplessness.

Day seven.

***

I'd done everything that the people who knew best had advised. For the short term, at least. The house had been boarded up as best as possible, save for the back door, which would serve as an emergency exit, should the need ever arise. We even had enough food to last a couple of weeks. That would be enough, surely.

I mean, how difficult could it be, to control an epidemic of slow-moving living dead people? They couldn't even *run*, for God's sake!

They still didn't know what was causing it. Some of the talking heads had been blaming that bloody American space probe and its unusual 'radiation,' before regular radio and television programming was switched off.

Seven days. That's all it had taken. If I'd been a religious man, I probably would've laughed long and hard at the irony in that fact.

I followed all of the advice. It's not as though I didn't. So I had no real reason to blame myself, even then.

I do though. I do blame myself and, I'll probably continue to do so, up until the end. I tell myself perhaps it's because I waited, as always. God knows it wasn't easy, trying to be strong for us both. Cathy was always the more emotional one, it never took much, so keeping her calm was a challenge. Particularly once people started leaving.

"George, are you coming?"

240

The voice belonged to Bob Smythe, our nearest neighbour, *nearest* being the operative word. Living in a country cottage had some benefits, peaceful isolation being one of them. It'd never been a bad thing in the past, now I wasn't so sure. I was in the middle of boarding up the front door at the time, you know, like the people who knew best had said. I looked out, between the wooden slats and though the glass. There was Bob, unusually unkempt, several days' worth of stubble darkening a face that already looked worn with stress.

Several steps behind him was his wife, Wendy. She looked as though she was taking it even worse than him. Her blonde hair was pulled back into a pony tail, although loose wisps hung in front of her face. Her eyes looked red and swollen, her cheeks streaked with tears. She was chewing at her fingernails.

God, I thought, *and I reckoned Cathy was handling it badly.*

"Coming? Coming where?" I asked him without opening the door.

"London," he said, running a hand through a tangle of greasy, unkempt hair. "There've been rumours that they've got proper bunkers down there. Underground stuff, meant for all those political bigwigs. Reckon we could try and force our way in."

"Rumours," I picked up on the first part. "You're going to travel half the length of the country because of a rumour?"

"Right now that's all we've got, George," I could sense a growing agitation in his voice. "Bloody country's falling apart. They reckon it's the same everywhere. We can't just stay here and wait."

"That's exactly what I intend to do." I tried to keep my voice low, for Cathy's sake more than anything. The last thing I wanted was her getting upset. Again.

"You're not serious, surely!" The agitation was starting to turn into frustration. "But you've got a *wife*!"

"Yes," I dropped my voice to a hoarse whisper, not wanting Cathy to hear any mention of her name. "And I think the best way of keeping her safe is to keep her here – *calm* – and to ride out whatever's going on."

"You're being *delusional*," he looked back at his own wife, still chewing away at her fingernails, she was beginning to sway back and forward, as though she might pass out at any moment. "Like that crazy bitch, Carmody."

"Agnes? What about her?" I asked. Agnes Carmody lived about a quarter of a mile along the road. A bit eccentric, to put it politely, she kept pretty much to herself, harmless enough.

"Gone and boarded herself in. Refusing to answer her door to anyone. Preparing for the impending Apocalypse, most likely. *Crazy.*" He emphasised this last word, as though he would've said the same about anyone with a view different to his own. I've always hated that, the way some people are so damned opinionated.

"Then you're probably going to think the same of me," I said. "Because that's exactly what I aim to do." I tried to make the words come out without sounding as mad as he suspected. It wasn't easy.

He looked at me, peering through the gap as though doing so would somehow change my mind. "You're *serious*, aren't you?"

"Very. I think we're better off waiting, rather than taking our chances. In the short term, at least."

"Short term?" He looked as though he was about to fall to his knees and beg. "And what about *after* that? What about when no one comes to help? You tell me what happens *then*, George."

I didn't want to think too hard about what he was saying. Perhaps I was afraid he'd actually make me rethink my decision, something I didn't want to happen. I needed to believe that what I was doing was right, for my own sake as well as Cathy's.

"*George*?" He asked again, when I didn't reply the first time.

"We'll take that risk," I answered firmly. I think I did a pretty good job, considering how much I was shaking on the inside. For a moment, Bob looked as though he was going to cry. Instead he took a deep breath and exhaled it again with a whooping noise, before continuing. "Then I hope you both make it. I really do. Goodbye, George." He turned around and began to walk back up the path. Suddenly, as though he'd just remembered something, he turned again fumbling with something behind his back as he did so.

"Wait! Open the door a second. At least take this." He shoved something cold and hard into my hand, pulling away again, as though afraid I'd reject his offer.

"A gun? Where the hell did you get this?" I looked down at the weapon I now held. It felt solid and weighty in my hand, the oiled barrel gleaming in the shards of light coming through the doorway.

"Standard issue. From my army days. I probably shouldn't still have it, but there you go. Safety's on. Only use it if you need to. You'll understand." With that he walked away again, without stopping this time. Back towards his wife and what was left of their lives, hastily crammed into a small car. He shook his head, still in disbelief, muttering to himself as he went.

After a couple of minutes they were both gone for good.

"Who was that, love?" Cathy came out from the living room where she'd been resting. She was rubbing at her eyes, to remove sleep or to wipe away at tears, I couldn't be sure.

"Just Bob and Wendy, dear," I said, tucking the gun into the back of my trousers. I've never considered myself a violent person and holding such an item made me feel dirty. "They're going away for a few days. Just until this whole mess has died down a bit." *Say anything*, I thought to myself, *anything to keep her calm.*

"You think it'll all be over soon, George?" she asked. There was a glimmer of something in her eyes, an expression on her face, faint, but definitely there. It looked almost a little like hope.

"Of course it will," I replied with a smile. *Say anything.*

I still thought I was doing the right thing, even then. God help me, I really did.

***

I'm still not entirely sure how it happened, or why she did what she did. Maybe she was sick of me being so damned over-protective, or maybe it was cabin fever. I'd kept the two of us locked away for eleven days by that point, so either explanation would be just as likely. I'll never know for certain though.

She was becoming visibly annoyed by the fact that I insisted on the radio being switched on, even though the nearest thing to a recognisable broadcast had ceased three days earlier, to be replaced with hissing static.

"Might as well turn it off," she'd said in an agitated voice. "The power supply will probably be going down soon anyway." Stubbornly I'd refused, stating that it was best to just wait and see. Waiting, again. Always waiting.

I was in the front room, dusting the photographs on the mantel. It seems stupid, given the circumstances, I know. Maybe in my own head, the carrying out of everyday tasks would help to maintain the illusion of normality.

I heard a clattering noise coming from the kitchen, the

sound of a plate or something being knocked over, followed by the back door slamming shut. I dropped the cloth in surprise and ran to where I knew Cathy had been busying herself. To the source of that noise.

Cathy was gone.

"Nononono—" I shouted aloud as I ran, pulling the door open to face the bright, almost forgotten sunlight, putting aside my own safety in the process.

Surreal. So surreal.

The garden looked so very pretty, with its neatly tended borders and its exploding rainbows of flowers. Cathy always did pride herself on her green fingers. There in the middle of it was Cathy, fending off something. Everything was a blur. Cathy screaming. Blood. Shambling creature, moaning. Screaming. Blood. Crying. A blur. Teeth locked somewhere in Cathy's arm. Screaming. So much screaming. So much blood. Everywhere. Blood. Pain.

The spell broke, the sound of her screams deafening, ringing in my ears.

Somewhere out the corner of my eye, something gleamed in that gloriously warming sunshine – Cathy's garden spade. Without thinking I picked it up and

(aim for the head)

swung it as hard as I could at the thing that still clung to her arm like a dog with a prize.

(head)

Bone gave out with a loud, dry crack, as the pan of the spade connected with the thing's head, matted hair parting in a bloody explosion of brain and skull fragments. It released its grip as though stunned and Cathy fell back, clutching at her arm. The thing staggered around almost comically, before slowly collapsing into a heap, blood still pumping like some viscous slime, staining the lawn.

"Cathy!" I screamed, dropping the spade as I rushed to my wife's side. Her eyes were closed and she was making a soft moaning sound, still holding her arm, trying to stem the blood that poured through her fingers.

"Let me look. Here, let me look." Cradling her against me, I gently pulled her hand away. Her forearm was mangled, a mass of raw, shredded flesh where the shambling thing had torn, first with its hands and then with its teeth. Instinctively, I removed my shirt and used it to bind the wound as tightly as possible. A crimson stain quickly bloomed on the cloth and began to spread its way outward.

Her skin was cold, clammy to the touch. *Oh God*, I thought. *Oh God, God, God.*

She turned her head and murmured, her breath shallow and warm against my cheek,

"Wanted... to go out... side. Needed... to be out... "

"Don't worry about that now," I said, scooping her up carefully into my arms, "You're going to be fine."

(tell her anything)

I turned to carry her back into the house, casting one last look about the garden as I did so.

There in the middle of that pretty lawn, filthy and ragged, fingers still clenching and clawing for something that wasn't there, was a familiar face.

It was Agnes Carmody.

For Cathy's sake as well as my own, I didn't scream.

***

By day fifteen the fever had well and truly taken hold. All I could do was try and make her comfortable and hope for the best.

***

- The problem is, it would appear, that there is a cycle of events evident, in which those attacked soon develop signs of infection. This rapidly leads to death, followed in turn by reanimation. There is a very real danger of this becoming a long-term problem. Of escalating out of control. The only real way of managing the situation – as callous as it may sound – is to dispose of those recently deceased, either by decapitation or cremation. There is no longer any dignity in death.

***

No dignity in death. That's what the talking heads had claimed, shortly before everything went completely out of control. I wish I could believe that wasn't true.

I tended to Cathy as best I could, all the time watching her deteriorate in front of me. After two days, her forearm showed clear signs of infection, where that woman – *thing* had attacked her. The flesh had begun to swell and blacken, the septic odour unmistakable. I cleaned the wound with what limited resources I had, I could feel my heart breaking as I struggled to accept that it was all in vain. The only saving grace was that she was too delirious to notice.

All the same, I did my best not to cry in front of her.

"George."

Hearing her voice took me by surprise. It was the fourth day after the attack, and for the most part, she'd been either sleeping, or murmuring incoherently. I leaned closer to hear her, stroking her cheek gently with my fingers as I did so.

"What is it, love?"

"That thing bit me, George. I'm dying."

"Don't say that, you're going to be fine," I was shocked by the frankness in her voice, as well as my own reaction to it. Not that it made any difference.

"Please George, don't lie to me," she sounded clearer, stronger than she had in several days. "I know I haven't got long. That's what they said on the news, isn't it?"

"They might've been wrong," I argued, wanting to deny the reality of what I was hearing. "You'll probably pull through soon."

She chuckled, it sounded alien, wrong somehow, given the situation.

"Poor, sweet George. Always in denial, always waiting for the right moment, even if it never comes." She tried to struggle into a sitting position, breaking into a fit of coughs as she did so. I reached across and put my hand in hers, gently wiping away strands of hair from her clammy forehead. "No," she assured me. "I haven't got long left, I know that and so do you. So there's something I want you to do for me."

After almost forty years of marriage, it should've been the easiest thing in the world to meet her gaze, but I couldn't do it. There was a raw, burning sensation behind my eyes, as the tears began to well up. I choked them back, wanting to be strong for myself as well as for her.

"Shush, now," I insisted. "You need your rest. You'll think more clearly if you get some sleep."

"You always could be a patronising pain in the arse. I've never told you so, but it's true." She still smiled, as if she enjoyed my look of surprise. "I'm thinking... perfectly clearly. You *know* what I'm going to ask."

I nodded my head, unable to speak.

"I don't want to be like that... that *thing* out there. I want you to make sure that doesn't happen. You'll do that, won't

248

you?" When I didn't answer right away, she repeated, "Won't you?"

"Yes."

"Promise me."

"Yes! Okay, God yes." I didn't want to imagine the possibility, but when I closed my eyes, I saw the shuffling thing that used to be Agnes Carmody, with its filth-matted hair and champing teeth. I thought of it chewing its way into my wife's arm, tearing away shreds of flesh as I beat it with the spade. I thought of it lying outside, its brain leaking out onto a lawn that was probably dying by now.

And I knew she was right.

"Good. That's good." Seeming satisfied with my response, she laid her head back against the pillow with a sigh, and closed her eyes.

Once I was certain she was asleep, I allowed myself to cry, just a little.

***

The gun still feels so very heavy as I pass it from hand to hand. It feels almost as though I'm handling a live grenade. In some respects, I might as well be.

She was right. I know I couldn't imagine the thought of walking around like that just as much as I couldn't bear the thought of *her* doing so. I love her so much – I always have – that I just couldn't stand it. I should maybe feel honoured that she's put so much faith in me. The faith to do what's right, when the time comes.

That doesn't make the burden any easier though.

I've been sitting watching her for the last hour now, just waiting. I watched her chest rise and fall softly as she slept. There was a faint gnawing sensation in the pit of my stomach, making me think of the dwindling supply of food in the cupboards. *More than enough,* I'd thought. Not for two, but for one perhaps...

I clenched my eyes shut and shook my head, hating myself a little for entertaining the thought.

Thankfully, the end came quickly. Her breathing became more laboured and after a little while, with little more than a brief twitch, stopped completely.

I didn't cry, I'd already got that out of the way. Instead I walked over quietly, kissed her once on the forehead, and sat back down.

There is no dignity in dying.

I keep telling myself I don't want my Cathy ending up like that: shuffling around, some mindless, undead *thing.* It helps, just a little. I look at her, lying there so peacefully, then I look down at the weighty chunk of metal in my hand. Gleaming and solid, with the power to make it all end.

'Only use it if you need to. You'll understand.' That's what Bob said to me when he left me the gun. 'I'd understand,' he'd said. And he was right, now I do. 'One of those leftovers from my military days,' he'd said, standard issue, apparently. I'd managed to open the chamber while idling away the time. I looked inside.

Two bullets. Not much, but enough.

No dignity in dying. That thought keeps going around and around my head. I hope it's wrong, I really do. All the time I'm thinking this, I'm just looking at Cathy, so peaceful, and waiting, waiting as always, even though I promised I wouldn't.

No dignity.

I'll just wait a little while longer and see what happens.

Lightning Source UK Ltd.
Milton Keynes UK
UKHW020643060519
342177UK00016B/3272/P